GUILT

and Other Stories

HAREKRISHNA DEKA

Translated by Mitra Phukan

SPEAKING
TIGER

SPEAKING TIGER BOOKS LLP
125A, Ground Floor, Shahpur Jat, near Asiad Village,
New Delhi 110049

Published by Speaking Tiger Books in paperback 2021

ISBN: 978-93-5447-086-8
eISBN: 978-93-5447-087-5

10 9 8 7 6 5 4 3 2 1

Typeset in Bembo Std by SÜRYA, New Delhi
Printed at Chaman Enterprises, New Delhi

Harekrishna Deka (born 1943) is considered one of the foremost writers of Assam with his novel experiments in modern and postmodern Assamese literature. He has distinguished himself in poetry, fiction and literary criticism. Belonging to the Indian Police Service, Assam-Meghalaya cadre, he retired from service as the Director General of Police. After retirement, he briefly edited the Guwahati-based daily *The Sentinel* and then became the editor of the prestigious Assamese magazine *Goriyoshi*. He has written more than thirty books. He received the Sahitya Akademi award in 1987 for his poetry collection *Aan Ejon*, the Katha award for short story in 1996, Assam Valley Literary Award in 2010 for his overall contribution to Assamese literature, and the Padmanatha Bidyabinod Literary award in 2015 for his contribution to Assamese poetry.

Mitra Phukan is an Assamese writer, translator and columnist. Her published works include four children's books, a biography, two novels: *The Collector's Wife* and *A Monsoon of Music*, several volumes of translations and a collection of her columns. Her most recent works are a volume of short stories, *A Full Night's Thievery*, and translations of works such as Gyanpeeth Awardee Birendra Kumar Bhattacharjee's *Kobor Aru Phool*. Her works, including her children's stories, have been translated into several languages, and are taught in colleges and Universities. She writes extensively on Indian music and theatre, both as a reviewer and essayist.

Contents

Translator's Introduction

The thirteen stories in this book are from a single writer's work. Harekrishna Deka, Sahitya Akademi awardee and highly regarded in the Assamese world of letters, is both a poet and a fiction writer. In addition, he is also greatly respected for his thoughtful, incisive essays on topics of social and literary importance.

The stories in this collection were written across several decades. The time span starts in the nineties of the last century with 'Guilt', and ends in 2015 with 'Love: An Essay'. They have been part of different anthologies and collections, and have also appeared in many widely read journals across Assam. Over the years, I have translated these thirteen stories as and when they appeared. Now that I am going through them again for the requirements of this volume, I am struck by how much the author's narrative style and artistic vision have changed over the years. These stories show the arc of a fine writer's work, from the early period to his later ones.

The writer considers himself to be primarily a poet, and came to the short story genre later. The first few stories have an intricate detailing of characters, their motivations, and actions. The situations are completely realistic, and the plotting is classic.

Over the years, there is a definite change in the way the narrative is propelled. The characters are still interesting, the plotting is still careful and logical, but the stories become more inward looking. There is more symbolism in them, and often the characters, while being believable, and individuals in their own right, also stand for something other than themselves. There is allegory, and there are extended metaphors. The traditional expectations of the classic short story remain very much in evidence even as the 'action' moves inward, to the mind. And yet the plot, development of character, of dialogue and the leading up to an ending that is often unexpected, remain the spine of the story.

The trajectory of these stories shows how a fine writer's thought processes evolve over time, influenced both by his own reflections and by the events taking place in the world around him. And living and working in contemporary Assam, no writer can fail to be influenced by the tumultuous happenings of the past few decades in this land. Some of these are, inevitably, mirrored in the later stories.

'The Captive' is one of the most widely anthologized Assamese short stories of contemporary relevance. Written from the point of view of a hostage, it describes, with empathy, the delicate relationship that grows between the captor and the captive. It is a kind of exploration of the Stockholm Syndrome, but it is more. There is no demonizing of the kidnappers—young men who believe in a particular ideal of what constitutes 'freedom'. The captive realizes that from the perspective of those who wish for a different kind of 'freedom', what they have done is not wrong in any way, and is completely justified. This is a deeply moving story, a character study as well as an examination of motivation, and a documentation of the terrifying times when kidnappings, extortions and killings were quite common in Assam.

It is almost impossible that a writer's profession and glimpses of his or her day job, should not be seen in his work, especially in fiction. Fiction, because the demands of plot and character, of dialogue and setting, need to be credible. Even if the work is based on imaginary events, the anchoring of it in a believable world so that there is a willing suspension of disbelief in the reader often has the writer delving into his own experiences in order to imbue it with verisimilitude. This is true of several of the stories in this collection, especially the earlier ones. As a senior police officer, the writer's exposure to aspects of crime and criminals yields some very interesting narratives. In 'Guilt', Durgeburhi's reaction when she is brought to the thana stuns the officer-in-charge. On the other hand, in 'Moustache', the story is developed in such a way that we see how somebody from within the system can manipulate it to his own advantage, smoothly and effectively, so that others remain unsuspecting of his motives until it is too late.

Several of these stories deal with characters from the underbelly of society. In 'The Temple', the unlikely friendship between a prostitute and a man afflicted with leprosy in the precincts of a temple propels the narrative forward. The contrast between the spiritual world that the temple, its priest, and its devotees embody, and the darkness that these two characters symbolize, is portrayed in stark relief

'Snake' is a story of a beautiful but neglected wife, and a man who is confident that he can attract any woman he chooses to with the force of his personality. The snake is a real snake, as well as a symbolic one. The sensitive narration explores the changing dynamics between the three characters with compassion and also humour. On the other hand, 'Madhusudan's Bridge' tells the story of why a particular bridge, old yet serviceable and still sturdy, has been named after a person about whom the people around know nothing. There is an element of the supernatural in it, of unexplained mysteries.

In 'Love: An Essay', the writer explores how hate can lie close to love, how love and hate are so closely allied, and also how love can so easily slip into a destructive, vicious, all-consuming hatred, how 'love', the word, can be used as a cover for an intense hatred. He also examines the complexity of patriotic movements, how love of one's country can degenerate very quickly into a hatred of the Other. This story is a sober look, beyond the emotionalism of 'patriotism', at the many inhuman acts that were committed in the name of love of the motherland during the Students' Movement of the eighties in Assam, and later. As always, the design of the narrative, with its cast of authentic characters echoes true incidents of the time, while always being true to the demands of the short story format.

With the passage of time, character- and plot-centric narratives give way to allegory and symbolism. We see the beginning of this in 'Yawn'. A middle-level politician tries to wrest power through devious means, but meets a sticky end. This is a complicated story, made engrossing because of the predicament which the protagonist finds himself in—of being unable to shut his mouth—and the stratagems he has to adopt to keep it all a secret.

The movement in the writer's works from realism to symbolism is something that has been of great interest to me as a long-term translator of Harekrishna Deka's short fiction. The contrast in the presentation between, say, 'Guilt', and 'A Mote in the Eye' is apparent. This later work is figurative, and a sharp, incisive social commentary on the times we live in. Yet the story, and its underlying theme, is couched in such a way that it is an engrossing narrative in its own right. There is humour and irony, but also empathy, bound together to present a clear-eyed view of society today. On the other hand, the irony and humour of 'Post-modern: A Story' aimed at literary pretentiousness and ambition, is encased within a format that has its own narrative force and logic. The characters, though bestowed with generic names, are real, and remind the reader of people whom one may come across all the time at literary meets.

There is a great deal of variety in these stories—of theme, settings and characters. Each tells the story of individuals from different milieus, with dissimilar concerns and lives. Together, they give a picture of this land, Assam, across distinct social strata, and in varied situations. And yet the characters and their dilemmas have an appeal that is universal, and will surely touch a chord in every reader.

'The Bestower of Death' takes the reader across different time spans, through decades. The incidents are both real and imaginary. The setting is absolutely realistic with the violence so common in Assam of the time. But this is not the main action of the story, which takes place, to a large extent, in the mind of the protagonist.

The way 'Romantic' unfolds is far from being the usual story of romance. It is layered, with the story of the birds building their nest forming an endearing leitmotif. But it is also the story of a boy, who unwittingly chanced upon a woman bathing in the open, in the nude. There is also another story, that of the narrator himself, who tries to speak his mind to a woman, but takes recourse to fiction and made-up stories in order to do so, possibly to hide his fear of rejection.

In 'Why Yudhisthir's Story Cannot be Told', the writer creates a plot that ends in a puzzle. It is like one of those games with two inconclusive endings. And yet the story complies with all the requirements that are demanded of the short story format. There is plot, of course, and a knitting together of believable incidents.

There is also a study of character and of logical and believable motivations. There is humour, and irony, too, and yet things are made to move in such a way that we come, finally to stand on the edge of a conundrum.

These stories were not translated in one go. Because of the time lag between translating the stories, the changes in the thought process of the author were very apparent to me, the translator. The style, too, differed. As the stories became more inward looking, the way of putting the narrative across also became more complex. These nuances and layers were very challenging to express in English, a language whose syntax differs greatly from Assamese. In addition, the complexity of these thoughts in the later stories required a particular kind of ironical expression. This was demanding in English, since subtle irony does not travel well across languages. And just as the author could not have written these later stories at the beginning of his career as a writer, I, as translator, too, would have found it even more difficult to put them across in another language when I was younger, without the maturity required for a proper reading of them. Yes, they were all challenging in different ways, as translation inevitably is. But it has been a very satisfying journey, all the more so because it has been such a long one.

Mitra Phukan
Guwahati, Assam

Guilt

A few handfuls of dhekia lie in front of Durgeburhi, their fronds wilting in the heat. It looks as though there is little hope that these last few bunches of fiddlehead ferns will be sold today. Durga sits in the shade of Badan's shop. Like her, a couple of others also sit by the roadside and hawk simple country vegetables and greens such as bamboo shoots, dhekia greens and kosu tubers. The railway crossing is nearby. The shuttle-train that passes on the tracks twice each day, morning and evening, usually pauses at this point for a couple of minutes. The passengers who alight from the train sometimes buy a few things from the hawkers here.

Her face is wrinkled, her sight has dimmed, yet Durgeswari cannot really be called 'old'. She is only about fifty. But in this neighbourhood, everybody calls her Durgeburhi, Old Durga. Some rowdy students of a nearby college come and sit on the gate of the railway crossing and create a huge commotion every day. They harass everybody in sight, and nobody can escape their unkind tongues. They plague one and all so badly that decent people avoid going on that road if those students happen to be around. Old Durga, too, has not escaped their attention. Actually, it is these students who are the authors of the epithet 'old' in front of her name, given to her even though she is only middle-aged. Once, one of them had mischievously taunted her. Durgeswari had given chase to the gang, cursing them and their ancestors mightily all the while. But after this incident, their ragging of her had become even worse. And now, every time they see her, they yell,

'In Shiva's matted hair,
Is Durgeburhi's lair!'

From the time of that incident, Durgeswari has been generally known as Durgeburhi.

Durgeswari appears at this spot very early every morning, though there is seemingly no need to arrive so very soon. But she appears before anybody else does to reserve for herself the prime spot where shopkeeper Badan's roof casts its shadow on the ground.

These days it is not really vital for her to come here and hawk vegetables. Her son, a strapping youth who has never seen his father's face, works as a peon in an office near their house. But Old Durga cannot give up her habit of selling vegetables in the market.

With the money that she earns in this manner, she hopes to bring home a wife for her son one day.

When the sun gets stronger, the shade afforded by the roof of Badan's shop shrinks in size. Still, it is not possible to follow the shadow and sit closer to the shop: Badan will be displeased. And who can sit in the fierce glare of this sun? The shuttle train has, in the meanwhile, left, so there is very little hope that these last handfuls of dhekia will be sold now.

The fronds cannot be stored, either, so Dugeburhi will have to utilize them for her own meal.

As Durgeswari prepares to leave, three shadows come to rest on her wares. Thinking perhaps the shadows belong to potential customers, she looks up, and gets an unpleasant shock.

Three men, dressed in khaki, are standing in front of her. Durgeburhi quakes inwardly whenever she sees men in khaki. However, screwing up her face to present a brave front, she mutters, 'I'm going, I'm going, after all I haven't built my house here, have I?' She gathers up the green fronds and puts them into her cotton bag.

At this, Constable Kalita speaks, 'Hey, old woman, wait a minute, our A.S.I. Babu has not come to evict you from here!'

Still, Durgeburhi does not feel at ease. What other motive can this daroga have for searching her out, if not to evict her? But the mystery of the policeman's presence there is soon explained.

'Old woman, do you remember the corpse that was found on the railway tracks over there, just about a hundred yards from where you are sitting now? Well, tell us—did you see the corpse?'

The old woman remembers. Yes, a corpse had indeed been found on the tracks very early in the morning, just the other day. The head had parted from the rest of the body, sliced clean by the wheels of a passing train. The old woman is about to answer, but something makes her pause.

Three college boys pass that way. They yell out lustily,

'In Shiva's matted hair,
Is Durgeburhi's lair!'

Durgeburhi begins to tremble. Is it caused by anger, or by some other emotion?

Certainly, the old woman had seen the corpse. And not just the corpse, she had also seen other events that had taken place.

On that day, she had got up at cock-crow, as usual, and, gathering together the leafy mustard greens that she had collected the previous day, had walked the two miles to this spot. On the way, she had crossed the community Puja pandal. There had been just a few days left for the Puja festival to begin. She had seen an image-maker busy painting the image of the goddess. He must have woken early in order to finish the remaining work on the image before the festival started. She had gazed with fixed intensity, not at the goddess, but at the ferocious aspect of Mahishasura, and at the clay likeness of the severed bull's head. Durgeburhi always found it difficult to believe that the severed, lifeless head of the bull, and the great Asura, were two facets of the same living being. She had, however, been gratified to see the wicked Asura's approaching death, caused by the wound in his breast inflicted on him by the goddess.

It had still been dark that morning when Durgeburhi

had reached Badan's shop. Thinking that it was pointless to set up her stall that early, she had gone behind Badan's shop to rest a bit. It was then that she had seen the incident take place. She had noticed a jeep come up very fast. It had stopped near the railway crossing. Two men had alighted hastily. Together, they had lifted something heavy from the back of the jeep. At first, she had thought it to be a sackful of salt, or something similar. On looking more carefully, she had realized that it was the body of a man. Before Durgeswari could fully comprehend what was happening, the two men had placed the body on the tracks. They had then returned rapidly to the jeep. Before Durgeswari had the time to notice any details about the vehicle, a goods train had appeared, and run over the body. She had distinctly seen the head being severed from the torso. The head had rolled away from the tracks.

Durgeswari was very disturbed by the sight. She had walked away in a daze till she reached the community Puja pandal once more. Only after a long time had she been able to gather her scattered wits together. The image of the bull, with its head severed by the avenging goddess, had reminded her, again and again, of the head on the railway tracks.

When, eventually, she finally returned to her stall, she had found the place crowded with people. The police had, in the meantime, removed the corpse. That day, the green signal for the shuttle train had been a long time in coming. It had remained at the crossing for quite a while. A large gathering of people had collected there, and she had been able to sell off her vegetables quickly.

Durgeswari is unaware of the length of time that has elapsed since she began to mull over these events. She returns to the present only when the A.S.I. shouts impatiently into her ear,

'Hey, old woman, why don't you say something? You are always here before anybody else. Did you see anything?'

Before she comprehends what she is doing, Old Durga finds herself saying, 'Yes, I saw it.' Only then does she realize what she has let herself in for.

The A.S.I. rejoices on hearing this, for is it not always extremely difficult to get an eyewitness to a crime? Durgeswari suddenly becomes very precious to him. Hastily summoning a constable, he orders, 'Go and get the Trekker, ask for it to be fetched here.' Turning to the old woman, he says, 'Don't you worry now. You will have to come with us to the thana. We shall drop you off at your house in the vehicle after we record your statement.' This last bit he adds in order to cheer her up.

Old Durga had only seen the corpse from afar, and that, too, in the dim light of dawn. But in the Trekker that takes them to the police station, the severed head of the corpse seems to come alive and dance in front of her eyes. She thinks she vaguely has a faint memory of its features. And she also remembers the head of the bull under the goddess's feet. Both the severed heads seem to whirl madly around as they dance in front of her mind's eye.

Durgeswari is produced in front of the Officer in Charge of the police station. The A.S.I. tells him,

'Sir, this old woman is an eyewitness. Her statement should be recorded, sir. We have managed to locate her only after a very long and difficult search.'

The chief asks her to wait on the bench outside his room. He will be able to record her statement after some time, as he is busy with some other work at the moment. Durgeswari quakes inwardly. She has never seen the inside of a police station before. The stench from the urinal behind the lock-up assails her nostrils. She plugs up her nostrils with her sador. What will the Chief Inspector ask her about the headless corpse? Who knows how long this affair will take. If her son, on returning from his office, finds her missing, he will probably give her up for dead. He will never come in search of her: he is not capable of that much resolution of character, fortitude, or stamina.

From some distance away comes the sound of a drum, as one of the Puja drummers begins to play it. Durgeburhi starts up on hearing its rhythm. There must be a Puja mandap somewhere near the police thana. Today is Sasthi, the day the image of the goddess is installed in the mandap. No wonder the drums are playing so insistently, hammering out a rhythm inside her head.

The old crone remembers, once more, the image of the goddess that she saw in the community pandal a few days ago. She remembers also the revolting face of the demon Mahishasura. Every year, she has, in her own mind, slashed at, and hacked to pieces the image of the clay Mahishasura. Once more, the head of the Asura seems to dance in front of her eyes. But along with that comes a face that belongs to her past. To the time, twenty-five years ago, when she had been a young girl. In fact, she remembers not one, but two faces.

Durgeshwari sees herself, a quarter of a century ago, in front of another Puja pandal, a container of kerosene in her hand. The bottle had been empty—there had been no kerosene in the market. She also carried a tiny packet of salt, and a bag which contained a little rice and some dal. She had looked at the image of the goddess, but, repeatedly, her gaze had wandered to the horrific representation of Mahishasura. In the tableau before her, the bull's head had been freshly severed by the force of the goddess's blows. Imagining this scene, the young Durgeswari had breathed a sigh of relief.

She had not realized how much time had gone by as she gazed at the tableau. On other days, she would have cringed with the fear that her husband, Mahesh, would beat her on the back with pieces of firewood. But that day, she had gazed for a long time at the image of the goddess before her. She had returned to reality only when the tiny new life growing within her squirmed in her belly.

While gazing at the goddess, she had also remembered the pock-marked face of her neighbour, the shopkeeper Ghono. Lately, however, he had become much more to her than a neighbour: the growing child in her womb reminded her just how much more. Her intimacy with Ghono had been a refuge for her, a shelter from the violent beatings of her rascally husband. A wave of nausea swept over her as she pondered on this.

She had returned home very late that night. On crossing the threshold, she uttered a piercing scream: the grotesquely severed head of Mahesh lay on one side of the bed.

It had not been a scream of fear. It was stage-dressing, a part of that plot which had been hatched between her and Ghono.

Eventually, however, the police had recovered the murder weapon—a hatchet—from under Ghono's bed. On being led away by the police, Ghono had perhaps wanted to express his feelings to her. Perhaps he had wanted to say, 'I shall return. Wait for me.'

He had never returned.

She had never wished for his return. Much before Ghono had hacked at his head, another blow had fallen on Mahesh's neck. Durgeswari had given him a sleeping draught and herself decapitated Mahesh. She had not thought it necessary to tell Ghono this. In the darkness, Ghono had given a blow to the already dead body. And now Ghono had gone to jail.

Well, let him. After all, he, too, was a scoundrel.

Durgeswari returns to the present at the constable's shout. 'Come on, the Daroga Babu wants you.'

Durgeburhi appears in front of the O.C. Her gnarled and wrinkled limbs tremble. The drums in the nearby Puja pandal pulse out their hypnotic rhythms unceasingly.

The O.C. asks her, 'Tell me, old woman, did you see the murderer?'

Once more, the relentless rhythms of the drums assail

the very core of her being. The severed heads of men and bulls gyrate together in front of her prematurely aged eyes. She feels suffocated by the memory of Mahesh's severed head. From her sunken, frightened mouth, the words rush out.

'Yes, yes, I killed him! I killed him!'

The Chief Sub-Inspector gapes at her, as though confronted with a riddle.

The Temple

Almost all the inhabitants of this small, practically rural town were glad on the day when the temple of the Devi got its own water supply. The town drew its importance from the temple. Bands of devotees came here from surrounding places. Numerous stories of the mercy of the goddess had, through constant repetition, grown to the proportions of a legend. Nobody tried to verify the truth of those stories now. They only believed that the goddess was all-powerful.

Therefore, when, due to the kindness of a generous patron, arrangements could be made for lifting water to the temple tank with the help of electricity, the people were satisfied. Only Hanu, who was against the scheme, was of a different mind. He was completely dissatisfied with the new arrangement.

All these years, it had been Hanu's responsibility to bring water for the devotees from the tank near the temple. He had earned a small amount by bringing the cool water to the travellers; this had been enough for his needs. But the necessity of providing comfort for hundreds of pilgrims had been of much more importance than retaining Hanu's means of livelihood. One man's job was sacrificed for the welfare of the greater number.

Yet even though he had lost his livelihood, Hanu could not leave the temple, for his life was entwined with it. Hanu was, no doubt, angry but even in his anger, he stood unbudging by the temple. The many hundreds of pilgrims who came here were perhaps unaware of it, but the stout priest who served this place of worship knew very well of Hanu's relationship with the temple.

Hanu's anger deepened when his stomach ached with the pangs of hunger. He would then scream out imprecations in an incoherent voice from afar. Yet there was nothing that the priest could do beyond stuffing his ears with cotton-wool. A few pilgrims who came to the temple for the first time would, on hearing such a voice, pelt Hanu with stones, much as they would a dog. But Hanu would scream even louder in his anger, making obscene gestures, so that there was no other solution except to disregard his ranting.

In appearance, Hanu was ugly. That was why nobody felt any sympathy for him. The most noticeable feature of his physique was his monstrous hunchback: it was as though his shoulders had bent carrying a weighty burden on his back throughout his life. Just below his flat nose, the curl of his upper lip seemed a little swollen, so that his similarity to the ancestors of mankind was accentuated. His very name—Hanu—was bequeathed to him by his ugly face: it was a shortened version of Hanuman.

When Hanu used to work in the temple, the priest, for his own selfish ends, showed him a little kindness and pity. Hanu would do a few chores around the house for the priest. Hanu knew about the priest's weakness for tasty dishes. He also knew of the priest's liaison with a certain washerwoman. These tales now streamed out of Hanu's mouth in filthy language. In this way, he appeased the hunger in his belly as well as the agony of his wounded body. For all Hanu's misfortunes had come thick and fast, and seemed now to have almost smothered him.

Just after he lost his job of carrying water for the pilgrims, he fell ill with a dreaded disease. His ugly face was disfigured even further by the ravages of leprosy which seemed to eat it away. A couple of fingers and toes fell off. Previously, he had been able to sit on the veranda of the temple. He now sat screaming under a Saptaparna tree, a milkwood pine, outside the temple courtyard. Many people thought he had lost his grip on sanity. But he was not mad.

On this day, too, as soon as the priest entered the temple early in the morning, Hanu started to shout, 'Hey! You eater of offal, you gigolo of that washerwoman! Who have you allowed into the place where I used to sit? You lump of rottenness, why don't you go to hell? I've poisoned the drinking water in your tank, you eater of other's castoffs!'

The priest blocked his ears for a while against Hanu's abuses. Later, unable to bear it any longer, he came out into the veranda. Fortunately, no pilgrim had arrived yet.

He said, 'Hey, Hanu, have you gone mad? Why are you polluting your mouth with such filthy language so early in the morning?'

On hearing the priest's words, Hanu's anger got inflamed even further. He shouted out obscene vulgarities. Covering his ears, the priest said, 'You miserable sinner, there seems to be no end to your sins. You are befouling the sanctity of the temple of the goddess. In your next birth, you sinner, you will be born a chandal, an Untouchable.'

Hearing the priest's words, Hanu laughed uproariously. He yelled, 'You fool, how am I better than a chandal now? Tell me whom have you allowed to sit in my place?'

The priest answered, 'Who am I to allocate a place for anybody? Isn't there a temple committee? Go and ask the committee. There is going to be a shop at that place. There will be a fair which will cover the entire field. The divine power of the goddess will be spread across the entire land. Devotional songs will be sung for seven days and seven nights. The Great Goddess is pleased, do you know that? The great Hara and Gauri, Shiva and Parvati themselves, will be conjoined in bliss. And the person who witnesses their union will enter heaven without having to leave his mortal body. This is not for an irreligious fellow like you—'

On being called irreligious, Hanu's anger flared up. He started to spit in the priest's direction. Seeing this, the priest was revolted. He quickly left the veranda and sought shelter in the innermost sanctum of the temple.

'Hey Hanu!'

Hearing the half-sympathetic, half-berating voice calling out for him, Hanu became magically calm. Wiping off the spittle that had sprayed his face when he had spat at the priest, Hanu turned around and saw Ahalya. Her face was garishly made up. A broad swathe of vermilion lay like a travesty on the parting of her hair.

Ahalya was a prostitute. Hanu listened to and obeyed only one person, and that person was Ahalya. She lived in the corner of a nearby market. She earned her living by trading her body for money. Hanu did not know how long she had been standing listening to him.

She said, 'For shame, Hanu, why do you pollute your mouth so early in the morning?'

Hanu asked, 'Well, Ahalya, how is it that you have appeared so early? Did you find no customer last night or what?'

Ahalya replied, 'And why should I not find any customer? That lot was bothering me throughout the night. They've come here to set up stalls at the fair, don't you know that?'

Hanu remembered. Yes of course, the priest, too, said that there was to be a fair. He asked, 'What fair, Ahalya? This is not the time for the usual fair.'

Annually, for a few days every winter, a fair would spring up here. But Hanu was surprised to learn of a fair at this time of the year.

Ahalya said jestingly, 'You idiot! Don't you know that the goddess has found a bridegroom? Our goddess will be leaving for her bridegroom's house!'

Her words made no sense to Hanu. He said, 'Oi Ahalya, don't talk nonsense now.'

Ahalya had not finished her jests. She continued, 'So is it not a sin if you pollute your mouth in the presence of the Devi? Now come along, I have brought some malpowas made with sweet chenichampa bananas for you to eat.'

Hanu moved back towards the Saptaparna tree. Ahalya followed at a little distance. Somebody had thrust some fresh stakes into the ground under the tree. Seeing this, Hanu's anger flared up again. But he controlled himself because Ahalya was with him. Going on a little further, they sat down beneath another tree. The fire in his belly cooled after he ate the malpowas.

The acquaintance between the unfortunate Hanu and the prostitute Ahalya was not a new one. It had grown over many years. In the beginning, in spite of being an ugly hunchback, Hanu had been a virile, mustachioed young man. A group of drunken men had, in frenzy, left Ahalya unconscious after raping her. If Hanu had not found her, she would probably have died. He had brought her back with him, nursed her to health, and had bequeathed her with a fresh lease of life. In return, one night after she had recovered, she had, during some intoxicating moments, given Hanu his first and only opportunity to prove his manhood. Hanu's experience of physical intimacy was restricted to that one night. As though it was a carefully hoarded sweet, his mind sipped even now of its sweetness. Because of his disease, Ahalya did not touch him anymore, but she brought him a few trifles every now and then. She looked after his needs as far as she was able to. Seeing his leprosy-ravaged limbs, even Ahalya secretly felt repulsed. She could understand a little of what the priest could not: the depth of Hanu's feelings that caused him to vent his unbearable emotional anguish on the goddess by blaspheming her. This was why she showed him sympathy even now. She brought him food and other necessities, and also some rags to cover his nakedness.

Hanu was of the opinion that the goddess of this temple has done him a cruel injustice. Otherwise why was he leading this agonizing existence, even though he had dedicated his life to her? When the image of the goddess was ceremoniously installed in the temple, Hanu's role was by no means a small one. In fact, Hanu believed that if he had not rescued her, the goddess would not be enjoying this kind of prestige today.

This had happened during the days when the tank behind the temple was being dug. It had been excavated many years ago, for the benefit of the people of the surrounding market areas, so that they could have access to a more convenient source of drinking water. Hanu, a stripling at that time, had had the opportunity of digging up a few spadefuls of mud in spite of his hunchback.

One day, while he was digging in this fashion, the tip of his spade clanked against what seemed to be a hard, ossified object. On retrieving the object, it was seen to be the image of a goddess carved in stone. A portion of the image's nose had been chipped and broken by the weight of Hanu's spade. Still, it was undoubtedly the image of a goddess. Hanu had brought the stone sculpture and entrusted it to the president of the market committee.

There was an uproar in the entire area as the news spread. Thousands of people streamed in to gaze at the image. It was not long before it was decided to establish a temple in front of the dug-out tank. The market committee shouldered the responsibility of setting it up. Gradually, the place of worship evolved from a straw hut to a tin-roofed house, and, lastly, to the present structure that rested on concrete pillars.

It became a place of pilgrimage for devotees. A fair was held annually on its premises. Though there was the upsurge of devotional feelings, along with the arrival of the crowds of pilgrims, there arose facilities for fulfilling their carnal desires. Shops selling liquor sprang up, shanties selling narcotics. A few prostitutes including Ahalya set up their business. After the blow that had disfigured the devi's nose, it became the custom to shield the image from the gaze of the devotees behind a muslin curtain. The pilgrims could not see the devi. Only the priests were entrusted with the responsibility of bathing and bedecking the image. The devi's unseen, merciful gaze from the darkened platform inside the temple became an attraction for the pilgrims. This mysterious unseen presence aroused the curiosity of the devotees, at the same time strengthening the bonds of their faith. Many tales of the devi's power spread to distant lands by word of mouth.

Hanu had been here at this very place since those early days, ever since the devi's frail beginnings. Earlier, he had been given the responsibility of sounding the bell that signalled the opening of the temple's door. Gradually, he had taken the responsibility of providing cool water to the thirsty pilgrims in exchange for a few coins. But today the very same Hanu was in this pitiable condition.

After eating the malpowas and the bananas that Ahalya had brought, Hanu's mind and belly both cooled down. He began to minutely question Ahalya about why the fair was to be held here at this time.

Ahalya replied, 'Well, I had come to talk to you about it. But the way you were screaming with rage, how could I bring up the matter? Come, I'll tell you about it now.'

Ahalya informed Hanu that a Shiva lingam had been found at a nearby hill which was avoided by most people for fear of snakes. It was not a man-made object. It was a natural lingam.

Hanu asked, 'Who saw it first?'

Ahalya replied, 'I can't say who saw it first. But the president of the temple committee has, it seems, had a dream that the lingam is the bridegroom of our devi. The goddess wants to stay with her husband. She will live for six months of the year with him, and six months here.'

The festival was to be held to celebrate the forthcoming union of Shiva and Parvati. The devi had made known through the dream that those devotees who worshipped her during the time of the festival would be freed from the bonds of grief, sorrow, suffering and illness. And they would be cleansed of all their sins.

Ahalya said to Hanu, 'The devi will remain seated on the same platform as her bridegroom for fifteen days, after which they will be put on separate platforms. The goddess will shower her blessings on the devotee who happens to be nearby during the time of their union. Hanu, if you can somehow manage to be near the image at that time, who knows, you may be cured of your sickness.'

Hearing this, Hanu laughed out aloud. Jokingly, he said, 'I had broken that heartless devi's nose unknowingly. She has punished me for that. Why should I go to see her display her powers? And you, Ahalya, will you be able to witness this sight? Your business will flourish during that time. I think you'll be very busy.'

Ahalya was shocked at his words. 'What is this madman saying? The goddess is listening, Hanu, don't say such things.' She moved hurriedly away before he could utter any more profanities.

The arrangements for the fair were made on a very large and elaborate scale. Many varieties of expensive muslin cloth arrived from the large markets of distant cities; hundreds of quintals of Joha rice, ghee, and so on arrived for use during the actual ceremony as well as for the ritual offerings of both cooked and uncooked food. Vast quantities of joss sticks and incense powder arrived. Groups of singers of devotional songs arrived from distant places and endless hymns reverberated continuously around the fairground. A never-ending variety of objects were ferried by bullock carts, hand-carts and motorcycles.

Displayed at the fair were beads and necklaces, sweatmeats and confectioneries, large varieties of cosmetics, utensils of brass and aluminium, vessels and containers of stone. Along with the printed anthologies of devotional songs and chants, illustrated sex manuals could be found, as were copies of the Arabian Nights. Making the fairground their destination came palmists, people who exhibited dancing bears and monkeys. There came magicians, wrestlers and even a circus. Stalls of greens, vegetables, star-apples and tamarind, brightly coloured beverages, snacks and savouries, thickly surrounded by buzzing flies, were set up. Peddlers selling mangoes and jackfruit arrived, so did barbers. And, day in and day out hundreds of devotees streamed in to gaze at these attractions.

The courtyard of the temple was always crammed with people till midnight every evening.

Hanu's cries and disturbances were overshadowed in this sea of humanity. Even Ahalya grew so busy professionally that she hardly had any time to look into Hanu's needs. However, Hanu did not suffer from hunger. Squabbling along with the other beggars for the half-eaten ritual offerings left behind by the pilgrims, he managed to eat till his belly was full. Yet he did not remain without creating a commotion. His anger increased because he felt neglected during the preparations for the festival. The pain of his deformed limbs doubled his irritation, and he started to vent his anger by screaming curses on fourteen generations of the priest's forefathers.

With this came gibbering about the devi's limbs and

body. Sometimes the priest would shout from afar, 'Hanu, you, you'll be damned.' But such imprecations did not bother Hanu, who would then start, instead, to scream out even louder. If he had not had an infectious disease, the pilgrims would probably have beaten him up and sent him off by now.

The day before the devi was due to leave for the home of her bridegroom, she had to be ceremonially bathed and beautified. She would be bedecked and adorned, and then installed in the palanquin. Hundreds of cheering devotees would pull the wheeled vehicle which was decorated like a chariot to the foot of the hill and from there be carried on the shoulders of the chosen few to the hilltop. Here the devi's bridegroom, taking on the form of a stone, was waiting with impatient eagerness for the arrival of the goddess, from whom he had been separated for so long.

Because the temple was closed, all the pilgrims crowded into the fairground on that day. During that time, the courtyard of the temple became silent. The priest and his helpers remained busy adorning the image of the goddess. The priest was afraid that Hanu would spoil this atmosphere of tranquil devotion. But when Hanu did not create any commotion, the priest and his helpers heaved a sigh of relief.

At this point, a problem arose. What was to be done if Hanu wished to pull on the chariot? Every person had the right to pull on the chariot, for the devi, it seemed, had spoken in a dream and commanded that nobody was to be denied the right to draw the chariot on that auspicious day. Arrangements were made accordingly. A separate rope was tied to the corner of the vehicle; if Hanu wished to pull, he would be able to do so on his own on that rope. The priest, however, hoped that Hanu, with his feelings of hate, would not come forward to pull on the chariot.

After working on all the arrangements in the temple till almost midnight, the priest, the members of the committee, and the other workers all went in various directions to rest for the night. The fair, too, broke up at midnight.

The next day, even before daybreak, the temple grounds were filled with people. The image of the goddess had been consecrated on a seat behind a curtain of muslin inside the chariot during the night. The devi was inside a beautifully decorated palanquin. Nobody was permitted to remove the curtain till she was united with her bridegroom.

At last, slowly, the journey began. Rending the sky with their shouts in praise of the goddess, the devotees began to pull on the chariot. With cymbals and drums, the bands of musicians walked, singing hymns. Conch-shells were blown, bells clanged out. Women made the auspicious ululation sound.

The members of the committee sat in the front of the chariot, while the priest sat holding the palanquin. It was a distance of at least four kilometers from the temple to the foot of the hill. The devi's procession paused at the slope for a while. The devi, in her palanquin, was brought down reverently from within the chariot. Even then the image was shrouded by a veil of muslin. People could not gaze upon her. Today, even the priest could not pay homage to the goddess before she was united with her bridegroom. This was the reason why the adornment had been completed on the previous day. The members of the committee respectfully shouldered the palanquin. The priest followed, and at a little distance behind him, came the devotees.

The journey was now a difficult one, through steep and thorny thickets. People did not usually venture up here for fear of snakes. Yet the frenzied pilgrims, oblivious to their physical hardships, scratched by thorns and subjecting their bodies to wounds, started their climb to the peak of the hill.

The nine-foot-tall stone was visible from quite a distance. From afar, it looked as though it was in the shape of a Shiva lingam. The devotees, eager to acquire virtues, discerned in this relic the manifestation of Maheswara himself. In their shrill voices they cried out Shiva's praise, and these, echoing round the hills, mingled in the sky.

On coming near the lingam, the procession suddenly halted. Hossanas and devotional songs died out, and a strange hush descended amidst them. The reason for this unreal silence was discerned by the priest himself. From where he stood some distance from the stone lingam, the priest could see a man sitting at the foot of the huge object. This person was sitting in a cross-legged position and staring steadily with wide-open eyes in the direction of the priest.

Approaching him, the priest recognized the man. In a terrified voice the priest shouted, 'Hanu, you monster, you fiend! What are you doing here? You miserable sinner, come away, come away from that place!'

Hanu gave no reply to the priest's words. He remained motionless and staring. A doubt crossed the priest's mind, and he went up to Hanu. He realized that Hanu had breathed his last quite a while ago. And what was that object that Hanu's lifeless hands were clasping to his body?

In the name of God! The priest did not take long to recognize the object at Hanu's breast: It was the image of the devi. Some time during the night, Hanu had stolen the broken-nosed image. In that case, what had they brought here in such a lengthy, elaborate and splendid procession? The priest's breast quaked. Running to the palanquin, he removed the curtain.

The palanquin was even then on the shoulders of the committee members. When the curtain was removed, it was revealed to the eyes of the crowd that what they had carried so devoutly in a procession was a slab of stone.

During the night Hanu had, unknown to anybody, kept the stone in place of the image of the devi, which he had brought with him.

Terror chilled the blood of all present. Suddenly, the palanquin seemed to weigh much heavier on the shoulders of the committee members. With a thud, they dropped it. At that moment, the fearful eyes of the devotees were drawn towards that huge lingam-shaped monolith. They saw the sunlight glistening on the stone. They observed that the motionless, lifeless stone was looking towards them, holding up its face to the sky with an indifferent gaze.

The crowd of terrified devotees started running down the hill as fast as they could. After they had all fled, there emerged a snake from the broken-nosed image of the devi that the dead Hanu clasped to himself. It slithered to the ground and vanished.

Madhusudan's Bridge

In the stillness of the night, a deafening sound woke up all the people nearby.

'The bridge has crashed, it's broken!'

Nobody knew exactly who shouted this out first. But immediately the last remnants of sleep fled from the eyes of the villagers, and a sense of urgency overtook them. Gathering up whatever they could lay their hands on, the young men of the village started running towards the bridge without even changing the clothes that they had slept in. The others followed.

The village stood on the edge of the highway. At any time of the day or night, a few accidents would occur there. Heavily loaded trucks in particular would often overturn on this stretch of road. The villagers would at once come running out to render assistance. It was as though they felt that it was their duty to help the victims of accidents.

Thousands of vehicles crossed Madhusudan's bridge every year. It was known to be a strong bridge, even though it was old and made of wood. The sturdy structure stood on stout wooden posts. Many accidents took place on both the approach roads leading up to the bridge. But till this day, no accident had ever occurred on the bridge itself. People said this was due to the grace of Madhusudan. The bridge had been built first; only much later did the people settle nearby. They had come looking for land by the roadside on which to set up their houses; now they were permanently established there.

Everybody admitted that the bridge had played a vital role in the development of the region. The area had been unhealthy, marshy and thickly forested. But after the bridge was built, this same area had been gradually cleared of forests and people had settled here. Fertile fields had taken the place of swamps and marshes. The region became particularly well-known for the cultivation of food grains.

A large variety of fish could be found around the huge pillars that supported the bridge. Shoals of fish, big and small, sheltered amidst the water hyacinths. On occasions such as Bihu and during festivals of the solstice, the people from the surrounding areas would happily try their hand at fishing with bamboo implements to trap the fish, with jakois, khalois and polois. A carnival atmosphere would spring up during these times. Sometimes, the vehicles that passed overhead, stopped to look at the merrymaking. If the catch was good, the drivers and handymen bought some fish to take away with them. Madhusudan's bridge was a witness to all these scenes of gaiety. For the youth who studied in the town's college, the bridge served as their clubhouse during their off hours.

In spite of the bridge being ideally placed for it, a suicide had never occurred here. It was not as though heartbreaking events had never taken place in the villages and hamlets nearby. Why, just six months ago, a girl named Jeuti from the southern part of the settlement trudged three miles to meet her death by laying down her head on the railway tracks there. Whereas she could have ended her life much more easily by jumping off from Madhusudan's bridge. Nobody leaped to his or her death from this bridge. People believed that to commit suicide here would mean showing disrespect to Madhusudan's sacrifice. However, nobody could say exactly who Madhusudan was or what his sacrifice had been. Various people related different stories and tales—Madhusudan was now a legend.

Today, when all the inhabitants of the nearby villages had been awakened by the loud noise, everybody realized that the sound was caused by the breaking up of the bridge, and nothing else. Without exactly knowing how it came about, the feeling that the bridge was soon to collapse, had taken root among the people. It would, they knew, collapse by itself. Without any obvious reason, the bridge would be rent asunder and, with a deafening noise, would sink into the bosom of the river Basumati. Perhaps, the hearts of the old as well as the young had been a little uneasy because this catastrophe had not occurred so far. It seemed that, unconsciously, they had gradually been losing their feelings of sympathy for the unknown Madhusudan. Exasperated, they had seemed to say, 'Well then, old wooden bridge, stay as you are. When the Public Works Department starts neglecting you, our descendants will forget to light earthen lamps in Madhusudan's memory. You will look pathetic next to the concrete structure that is being built over there. Then only the swirling eddies of the river Basumati will walk over you. Who wants to see this bridge, which is associated with the valiant Madhusudan in such a weakened state?'

The collective will of the people seemed to say that this should not happen. Just as the spirit of Madhusudan had protected the bridge so far, so surely he himself would take away this structure before it became too ramshackle. Madhusudan would not allow his bridge to stand beggar-like in front of the mighty concrete structure. Work on the big concrete bridge was progressing at such a speed that it seemed it would not be long before it was ready for use.

Nobody knew who first called the concrete structure the 'Big Bridge'. Now the entire public called it by that name. Perhaps somebody gave it that name to differentiate it from Madhusudan's bridge. By the time the people realized that by calling it the 'Big Bridge', they were implying that Madhusudan's bridge was small, it was too late to mend matters. By then also, it was thought that Madhusudan's bridge would one day collapse by itself for the sake of keeping its self-respect intact. Nobody could logically explain this astonishing belief. But it probably arose out of the hope that the reverence accorded to Madhusudan's soul would be best preserved in this way.

Therefore, when the noise was heard in the dead of night, everybody was prepared. And, instead of a feeling of fear, a wave of relief passed over their hearts. With these emotions in their minds, everybody came and stood near the bridge. On other occasions, the women, children, and the aged would have stayed in their homes, as it was very late. Only the able-bodied young men would have ventured out. But on this day, girls and boys, old men and women, mothers with babies in their arms, all came out and crowded around the banks of the river Basumati to see this unnatural occurrence.

It was observed that Madhusudan's bridge had collapsed spontaneously in the centre. Yes, exactly in the centre. A big supporting beam had overturned, and the portion of the bridge that had stood over it had been submerged underwater. Floating on the river were a few planks that had been torn off from the bridge.

Just as everybody had imagined, Madhusudan's spirit had protested in this manner against the engineers and the overseers of the Public Works Department. The people bowed their heads at the sight. A woman had brought along a few earthen lamps. These were lit and placed at the head of the broken bridge.

But on the banks of the Basumati, another sight revealed itself to the astonished gaze of the viewers. They saw that a white car stood waiting on the moonlit shore. Its body seemed to be still quivering. A few from the astonished crowd surrounded the car and peered inside. They saw a young man with his hands still on the steering wheel sitting in the driver's seat. His hands were trembling so violently that even the wheel shook. On the back seat, an old man lay on his side, with his head on a pillow. It was impossible to say whether he was asleep or awake.

Why should everybody be so astonished at seeing the car? After all, vehicles ply on this road by the hundreds around the clock. But the people were surprised to see the car which was, so to speak, an eye witness to what had happened to Madhusudan's bridge. Various questions were asked by the curious onlookers: where had they come from, where had they stopped, had they seen the actual sight of the bridge collapsing, did they need any help, was he asleep, the old gentleman who lay on the back seat?

The young man on the driver's seat was not prepared to answer all these questions. Swallowing hard he said, 'We have managed to escape by the skin of our teeth. Just as we were approaching the crossing, such a loud noise rent the air that I thought the car would fall into the river with us inside. How did the bridge break up without giving any hint of a warning? My insides are still shivering. I wonder what has happened to grandfather. He suffers from a heart ailment.'

One or two voices from the crowd asked, 'Why have you come with an elderly person so late at night like this? It is better to travel by daylight, you know.'

The driver replied, 'No sirs, we had scheduled our arrival at our destination for the evening. The car gave some trouble on the road. There was no workshop at the spot where it broke down. I went by truck and brought a mechanic from a place twelve miles away, and so we were considerably delayed. We would have halted for the night somewhere, but Koka, grandfather here has to be on time to reach a certain place tonight. God, a big accident has been averted.'

The gathering consoled him, 'Don't be afraid. This bridge is guarded by a deity. The deity has protected you. So many accidents have occurred on the road, but no such accident has ever happened on the bridge itself.'

The elderly man in the back seat had awakened at the sound of the crash; he was merely resting now. He had listened to the talk around him. Now he enquired, 'What is this place?'

'This is Madhusudan's Bridge, grandfather', replied a voice. People imagined that the name of the bridge was more likely to be recognized than the name of the place itself. It was almost a habit with the local inhabitants to speak of the place as Madhusudan's Bridge.

On hearing the name, the old man suddenly sat up. The youth who had been driving said wearily, addressing the senior as his grandfather, 'What is the matter, Koka? Don't sit up so suddenly like this, you might hurt yourself.'

The old man replied, 'It's my heart that is a little weak. My bones are still strong.'

Most of the curious crowd, in the meantime, had moved away from the car. There was plenty of work for them to do. The PWD office had to be informed about the collapse of the bridge. A couple of youths got ready to go there by bicycle. To warn the coming motorists of danger a few youths posted themselves at both ends of the bridge with red flags and lanterns. In the meantime, several vehicles had roared to a stop. Two or three lads went in search of pieces of cardboard. On these they would write, 'Road Closed', and put them up on both sides of the broken bridge. A few went in search of big boulders. These they would pile on both sides of the bridge so that nobody could climb the shattered crossing even by mistake. Some set forth in search of the owners of the small wayside stall which sold tea and betel nuts so that arrangements for refreshments could be made for the passengers and drivers of the stranded vehicles. A few more went to look for boats, so that those who wished to cross the river could do so on these.

Without listening to his grandson's words of caution, the old man alighted from the car and stared fixedly at the broken bridge for a long time. Amazement was written on his chubby countenance. 'Remarkable! Astonishing!' he murmured.

The young man had followed his grandfather, but he remained gazing at the old man's face. He failed to comprehend the meaning of his mysterious words. He was still shaken by the bridge collapsing just as he was about to drive on it. His nervousness had only subsided when the people from the nearby villages had come running and had talked comfortingly to him. However, it appeared that the people were talking in riddles! They did not seem to have any feeling of fear or anxiety in the face of such a calamity. The way they were behaving, it would seem that they were out to participate in some religious festival.

He was also surprised at his grandfather's behaviour. He had been in such haste to reach his destination that he had not waited even for a day so that his car could be sent to the workshop and they could travel in a more leisurely manner. He had been very restless too, when time had been wasted by the breakdown on the way. And now, after having escaped an accident by the skin of his teeth, not only did he show no signs of fear, it was as though he were actually reluctant to leave the place. He seemed to be waiting here, as though something was attracting him to the place.

Just as the young man was about to speak to his grandfather, a man with a lantern in his hand approached them and said, 'Respected Sirs, come this way. Have a cup of tea. The shops have been opened. Your throats must be parched, come and refresh yourself.'

Along with his grandson, the old man followed the unknown person to the tea-stall. This turned out to be merely a temporary shelter, with a bamboo fence around it. Inside were two pairs of small tables and benches. A couple of glasses of tea were kept on the table in front of them. The other bench was occupied by two or three others. They seemed to be the drivers or handymen of the waiting trucks.

Just outside the shop, two halves of split bamboo

were nailed together over a couple of posts to provide a makeshift seat. A few people were sitting there and relating, with many embellishments and exaggerations, the story of the bridge's collapse. Even though the incident had taken place only a short while ago, they were already colouring it with their own imaginations. Drivers, handymen and now a few stranded passengers of trucks and other vehicles formed a curious group of listeners. The enthusiastic storytellers had already imbued their tale with a supernatural atmosphere.

The owner of the tea-stall approached the old man and his grandson. He said, 'The car which was near the bridge when it broke up was yours, wasn't it? You must have got quite a shock. But there is no need to be frightened: the bridge is guarded by a deity who had doubtless looked after you. The guardian angel of the bridge has never allowed any unholy incident to take place there. He has taken his bridge back unto himself, with you as witnesses. Now that deity is a very holy being—he does not allow even a hair on a person's head to be harmed. He took away the bridge because he was annoyed.'

The shopkeeper was a very talkative man. The youth saw that his grandfather was eagerly drinking in his words, tapping on his own head all the while. The youth could not make out whether his grandfather was tapping his head out of sheer habit, or because he was impressed with the shopkeeper's words. He himself, however, was impatient to leave the place as soon as possible.

The loquacious shopkeeper brought up the subject

again, 'Ever since the new bridge was started over there, we have been waiting for something like this to happen. The PWD people have been shamefully neglecting this bridge after work was started there. The haughty tone in which they have been speaking—isn't it but natural for this bridge's deity to get annoyed? They say that this dates back to a very long time, that it is embarrassing for such an ancient bridge to be seen around these days. Now we will watch the fun. That new bridge is yet to be completed. This bridge has borne mighty weights on its bosom. Now it's all over. Let us see how the PWD gets across all these vehicles, hundreds of them, every day and every night!'

The old gentleman now spoke up, 'Of course the bridge had become very old. With proper maintenance, it may have lasted for some more time. However…' he hesitated, but did not complete his sentence.

Looking at the tea-shop owner, the youth asked, 'Why is this bridge called Madhusudan's bridge?'

His grandfather looked as though he were about to say something, but the shopkeeper interrupted, 'I don't really know. Apparently he was some noble soul. I have heard it said that long ago when the bridge was being built, it was in danger of collapsing. Madhusudan suddenly appeared and sacrificed his life to save the bridge. His soul left his body in the waters of the Basumati. But his spirit has become the guardian deity of this bridge.'

'Don't you know who that person was, or where he had come from?'

'These villages have come up long after the bridge was built. Our ancestors had not yet come here at that time. We have heard of these things only in a vague sort of way. The bridge was built at the time of Independence, when these places were marshy and waterlogged. Human habitation started here about thirty years ago.'

The old gentleman suddenly got up. Looking at his grandson he said, 'Come, let us go down and touch the waters of the Basumati.'

He started to walk towards the river. The youth realized that it would be futile to try to stop the old man. So, after paying their dues at the tea-stall he set off after his grandfather. On reaching the river bank, the old man washed his face with a little water from the flowing Basumati. For a long time, he stood and gazed at the broken bridge. Turning to his grandson he said, 'When this bridge was built I was here. The very person whose death we are on the way to condole, was the contractor who built this bridge. Long-forgotten happenings. But look at the amazing coincidence! On the way to mourn the contractor's death, we have become witnesses to the last moments of the bridge he built.'

Curiosity and amazement were written on the face of the young man. His grandfather presumably knew about Madhusudan. He asked, 'This Madhusudan that everybody here keeps talking about, was there actually anybody by that name at that time?'

Without making any attempt to satisfy his grandson's curiosity, the old man stared fixedly at the flowing waters of the Basumati. The first rays of dawn had touched the river. After all this time, it seemed as though he was seeing Madhusudan's face in the glimmer of the waves.

How old had he been then? Perhaps twenty-two or twenty-three. His mother had died when he had been quite young. When his father too had died, the contractor, Hemnath, had brought him as a homeless youngster to this place. He was given the work of supervising the labourers. He was to keep an eye on the work done by them.

The contractor had been a close friend of his father's. He had said, 'Stay with me for awhile, Mahananda, and learn the ropes. If you stick to this work, you will be able to stand on your own feet one day. Who knows what is written in your fate? Your wheel of fortune may take a turn for the better right here.'

This prophecy had truly been fulfilled. But that was much later. Before he could become independent, he had to labour long and hard. But success had come his way at last and he had prospered. However, for the contractor Hemnath the wheel of fortune had been reversed. None of his children had turned out well. His strength had failed. He had fallen prey to various illnesses and ailments in his old age and, enfeebled, he had given up his life. This journey was the result of receiving news of his death.

Who could have foreseen that this bridge was to be the cause of Mahananda's rise in life? For that matter, who could have known that another man's life-story would assume a mythical proportion here?

The man had arrived with all the force of a comet while work on the bridge had been in progress. Dressed in shabby clothes, he had disheveled hair, reddened, wild-looking eyes, and a huge, unsteady body. Nobody knew where he had come from. His appearance seemed to say that he had just that very moment had his fill of a large quantity of potent liquor. Hemnath, the contractor, had been busy explaining the work required to some labourers. The stranger had lurched up to Hemnath and grabbing his arm, had said, 'Well, you bloody contractor! Thought I wouldn't be able to find you, eh? You have sucked up all the money in the contract, and now you're planning to feast on the work here…'

His wild look, hoarse voice and the way he clutched his arm had proved too much for Hemnath. He had started trembling.

Looking at Mahananda and the labourers, the stranger had said, 'I, Madhusudan, have been in jail for the cause of Independence. If the country had not become free, doubtless they would have hanged me. This bastard of a contractor knows this. The government freed everybody at the time of Independence, otherwise…After I came out I saw bloodsuckers all around, everybody has snatched up whatever was around, everybody is now a leader. These contractors have suddenly become patriots, it seems. And we, who have served out our sentences in jail, fail to find any work; we have had to tighten our belts. Our names are down on the jail lists. Our bodies have been broken and people like this contractor are enjoying themselves after sending us to jail. During the days of the British rule, these were the ones who reaped the benefits. And now also, they are feasting off the fat of the land.'

Grabbing hold of Hemnath's shirt, he had lifted him by sheer brute force a foot off the ground. Looking at him with eyes that glowed like live coals, he had said, 'I shall stay here. You will have to give me work. Do you think that you will build the bridge with rotten wood, and pocket the loot? That can never be. If there's any trickery this time, by God, I'll hang you from the posts of the bridge.'

At that time, Mahananda had not been able to fathom the relationship between Hemnath and the stranger, nor could he make out how long they had known each other. Of course, a mere overseer had no call to know such things. But the contractor Hemnath had given the stranger work. The contractor greatly feared the man. Madhusudan had never done a stroke of work. His whole day would be spent shouting and invoking curses on Hemnath's ancestors. Posing as a know-all, he had caused unrest among the labourers. He would obstruct the work in progress. Nobody could say anything, for all were afraid of him. He would force them to refill land that they had already filled, he would uproot posts that had been laid, put new ones in their place; he would minutely examine the wood brought in to construct the bridge, and then create a commotion, insisting that the wood was rotten. Several times he had actually thrown away the logs into the river, saying that they were useless. On a few occasions he had even taken the logs from the building site and used them as fuel.

It had become obvious that Hemnath was becoming fed up with Madhusudan's antics. But what was he to do? His terrifying looks, foul language and threatening behaviour had completely demoralized the contractor. And though Mahananda had been young, he had realized that Hemnath had a feeling of guilt about something.

One day, when the work on the bridge was nearing completion, Hemnath had called Mahananda aside and said, 'I have bagged a big contract near the Naga hills. This work will have to be finished quickly now. But don't let that wretch know anything about it. From tomorrow start hurrying up the work and finish off the bridge as soon as possible.'

The contractor had started to work in a hasty manner on the bridge, trying to patch up the remaining tasks as soon as possible. On seeing this haste, Madhusudan had become suspicious. His interference with the work had increased. One day he had fallen on the man working on the railings of the bridge, and had mercilessly beaten him up. He had started to yell, 'You bastard, is this a railing you are building, or a fence? This half-baked contractor is creating a man-trap here.' With brute force, he had kicked at the railing. At the very first blow, the railing had broken off and fallen into the water below. Unless one had exceptional strength, it was impossible to break apart a newly constructed railing of strong wood with a single blow. The men at work on the bridge had cowered with fright.

On that day, however, Hemnath the contractor had become very angry. Looking at the labourers he had shouted, 'What are you looking at? What the hell are you looking at? How long will you suffer that monster? Why don't you get together and thrash him?'

On hearing the contractor's words, perhaps a feeling of bravado crept into the minds of the workers. Together, they gathered whatever weapons they could find handy—pieces of wood, bits of stone—and started attacking that huge form. If Madhusudan had been an ordinary human, he would doubtless have perished under this combined attack. But he was such a strong fellow that he gave as good as he got, and had even wounded a few of his attackers. But how could he, alone, have fought with so many? Covered with blood, in the end he had walked off unsteadily.

After this incident, Madhusudan had not been seen around for a few days. In the meantime, Hemnath had been working to finish the bridge as soon as possible. He had become very impatient those last few days. That year the monsoon had come quite early, and the rain had halted progress of the work on the bridge. He would feel thankful if he could somehow, anyhow, finish the work and depart with his money before the heavy rains set in.

The work on the bridge was completed at last. An officer of the government department checked the work and found it satisfactory

Arrangements were made to hand over the bridge to the government department. Hemnath arranged for two trucks to transport his men and materials to the new work-site. After this, he departed in a satisfied frame of mind.

However, there had been, that night, a torrential downpour of rain. On other nights, the labourers would have stayed up late, making merry and singing. But because they were scheduled for an early departure the next day, and because of the heavy rains, they had all had their meals and retired early to sleep in their makeshift shacks. Mahananda had a small hut to himself; that evening he, too, had gone to bed early as there had been nothing for him to do.

Very late at night, Mahananda was suddenly awakened. He was unable to make out the time. The sound of the rain had stopped outside. But he was surprised to hear, at that hour of the night, the sound of footsteps outside. It seemed somebody was repeatedly walking back and forth on the road leading up to the bridge. Softly opening the single matting door, Mahananda stepped out. The rain had stopped, and the sky had cleared somewhat. A faint haze of moonlight lit up the countryside. By this light Mahananda saw a man with a bundle in his hand walk up to the bridge. He placed the bundle near the first supporting pillar. Then the man turned back the way he had come, and paused. Even though Mahananda could not see the man's face very well, he realized by his manner of walking and by his general appearance, that it could only be Madhusudan. Undoubtedly, Madhusudan had also seen him. Changing his course, he approached

Mahananda. In a hoarse voice, he said, 'Go away from here immediately. Go back to sleep. I will smash Hemnath's bridge tonight. If you raise the alarm, I will finish you off, is that clear?'

Mahananda was unable to speak. Madhusudan had looked fierce and grotesque: his face was still swollen from the beating that he had received a few days earlier. It did not take Mahananda long to recognize the packets that had been placed near the pillar: they were packets of explosives. Mahananda had seen them a couple of times in the stone-quarries. His gaze locked on those packets, and his legs started trembling. In spite of Madhusudan's threat, he was unable to move from the spot.

Looking at the packages Madhusudan said, 'I have stolen these from the stone-quarries. One side of the bridge will be blown up quite nicely. I shall not let Hemnath go away from this place in a hurry. He must be taught a good lesson. I'll be satisfied only when all his money has been used up in repairing this broken bridge. You go off now, go back to sleep, come out only when you hear the explosion.'

Swallowing hard, Mahananda managed to call after the departing Madhusudan, 'Dada, why are you out to do this?'

On hearing the appellation 'dada', 'brother', Madhusudan stopped abruptly. His expression softened somewhat. He returned and, standing before Mahananda, looked at him for a while with a penetrating gaze. An anguished sound was wrenched out from him, as if he had been bottling up some deep pain inside his being. Sighing deeply, he said after a long while, 'Since you have asked, then listen. But before that look at my body.' Saying that he had taken off his shirt. Mahananda observed several deep welts on his back. Seeing the skin stretched tight across the gashes, Mahananda understood that they had not been upon Madhusudan's body from the time of his birth; rather they had been acquired during his lifetime.

'These scars have been put on my back by the British police, do you understand? The police station was near our house. Once, before my very eyes, the chief officer of the station shot dead three young boys as though they were dogs. To avenge that deed, I threw a bomb at the officer's house. He was not killed. Instead, his son was wounded. I was caught. This Hemnath knew that I threw the bomb. The police officer arrested him and Hemnath told him about me. Seizing me the officer said, "You have wounded my son. You will be punished for that in a way that you will remember all your life." How could I know that his son would be hurt? Sure, I felt sorry for the boy. The officer was the one who should have been killed. But in his place a small boy was wounded. This is what sometimes happens. But do you know what that officer did to me? You'll not believe me if I tell you. See for yourself.'

Saying this, Madhusudan took off his remaining clothes. Mahananda's eyes fell on the lower part of his naked body. For the first time, he understood Madhusudan's inner torment. His heart cried out and he closed his eyes in pain. When he finally opened them, Madhusudan had covered himself again.

A long sigh escaped Madhusudan's lips. 'Yes, this is my condition. I am alive. But my life has no meaning. That police officer took away my manhood. Cruel and vicious that he was, he inflicted this torture and said, "You will not die, but till the end of time you will remember the lesson you got for hurting my son." No, I did not die. I was imprisoned. Besides the bomb-throwing incident, many other imaginary charges were brought against me. I got a long sentence but that was nothing. My inner torment was greater. I thought if I could get out of jail, I would take my revenge on the officer. But when I came out, I learnt that the monster had already died in a car accident. But this Hemnath is left. He has become prosperous with his shady deals. That's what he makes in the name of contract work. People like Hemnath reap unfair profits even after Independence. I shall not take away his life. But in return for the enmity that he has shown me, I shall not let him live in peace.' Madhusudan was panting from the strain of talking for such a long time. Mahananda was no longer surprised by the feeling of revenge and animosity that had been bottled up in Madhusudan's breast.

Unable to speak, Madhusudan paused. After a while, he said again, 'Mahananda, go away, go to bed. You are not my enemy. Don't put obstacles in my way.'

It seemed that he was suppressing a cry that wanted to be let out. Slowly, Mahananda went back to his makeshift hut and closed the door behind him. But he was unable to sleep. His heart hammered loudly in his breast.

Mahananda lost all track of time. He waited fearfully for the sound of an explosion. It seemed as though time had stopped. At last, he heard a sound. It was not, however, the sound of an explosion. It was a shrill, piercing scream, 'Ma-ha-nan-da!' Madhusudan was shouting out his name.

The voice had come from the river under the bridge. This time he clearly heard Madhusudan's voice, 'Mahananda, come, come quickly! The post of your bridge will break down with the weight of these leaves! Call your men, the bridge is going, hurry.'

Looking down, Mahananda had seen danger. The water in the river was rushing in a mad torrent. The rushing, swirling cascades seemed to hiss like angry serpents. The bridge seemed to move. Bracing himself against the central pillar, Madhusudan was trying to force back a huge mass of water hyacinth with all his might. Only his face and head were visible. His whole body from the neck downwards was buried under the weight of the leaves.

Mahananda was bewildered. The same Madhusudan who had been prepared to blow up the bridge was now fighting with all his might to save it from a natural calamity! The packets of explosives that he had brought with him had probably been swept away by the current of the flooded river.

Mahananda ran and woke up some labourers. Arriving on the scene, they saw how Madhusudan, defying death, battled with the thick, all-enveloping growth of hyacinth leaves. Inspired by his courageous behaviour, the labourers, too, climbed down to the bosom of the river to attack the fiendish vegetation.

Due to the hard work of all, the bridge was saved. Bit it proved impossible to rescue Madhusudan from the depths. Nobody knew where the Basumati's current swept away his body. Mother earth is also called Basumati. Into the lap of this Basumati, Madhusudan had vanished for ever.

After the incident, Madhusudan became a revered figure in the eyes of the very workers who, a few days ago, had beaten him up till he had been at death's door. Nobody realized why Madhusudan had come to the bridge that night. Mahananda had not deemed it necessary to tell anyone about this. It became generally known that Madhusudan had saved the bridge from the devastating current of the flooded river.

The workers lit hundreds of earthen lamps for his soul. That had been the beginning. Gradually, Madhusudan's name had acquired the proportions of a legend. The story changed shape as it was passed around from mouth to mouth, and he became intimately connected with the bridge itself.

Later, many technical flaws in the bridge's structure had come to light. Many aspects of safety had been neglected for the sake of speed. Perhaps, if Madhusudan had not saved the bridge by giving up his life, it would have collapsed in the very first flood of the river. Afterwards, those defects had been corrected, and the bridge had been made quite sturdy. In addition, two guide-bundhs had been built on both the banks. As a result, thousands of vehicles had crossed safely over the strong structure.

Sometime later, Mahananda's life had taken a different turn. Fortune smiled on him. He enjoyed a prosperous, full life. The reason for his success in life was his integrity. But because of the scandal that had arisen from this work, Hemnath lost the job in the Naga hills. The last days of his life had been very sad, as he had become destitute and an invalid.

The old man recalled these almost-forgotten days of his early life. For a long while, he gazed at the muddy waters of the river. He did not think of relating the surprising tale to his grandson. Madhusudan had been immortalized in the collective memory of the people here. He did not wish to pull down this hallowed memory to earth by relating mundane details of Madhusudan's life and times. The young man was looking curiously at his grandfather, who had been silent so long. The old man met his eyes and seemed to come back to his senses. He said, 'Come, let us go back to the car. It is morning already. We shall go back and take the other route. It will be late by the time we reach Hemnath's house. I wish to spend some time with his children and grandchildren.' The two returned to the car. The youth sat with his hands on the steering wheel. The old man sat at the back.

Starting the car, he asked again, 'You have not told me who Madhusudan was.'

The old man replied, 'Haven't you heard what these people here have been saying? He was a noble soul. That should be enough. What is the use of wanting to know the real man? Do you know what has pleased me immensely? These simple people have given so much value to Madhusudan's sacrifice, and kept his memory alive.'

The car moved forward. This time, the youth remarked, 'One point displeases me. This bridge was built when you were still a boy. You are now an old man. The importance of this road has increased considerably since then. A concrete bridge should have been built here long ago. Only now has that taken shape. And it did not seem to me that the work there is progressing at all fast. These people seem quite content to be living in the past. It's a good thing the old bridge has collapsed. Otherwise, these people would have forgotten to look to the future.'

The old man did not reply. He kept gazing at the young man sitting in front of him, who, though his grandson, and part of his own flesh and blood, seemed to be an inhabitant of a different world altogether.

The Captive

He had been cycling since afternoon. It was now almost dusk. He felt extremely tired.

If only he could rest for a little while…

It appeared that the youth who was cycling beside him understood what he was feeling. Suddenly raising his hand, he gestured him to a stop. The youth also got down from his own bicycle. As he alighted, he noticed the picturesque surroundings. The place was near the highlands. A stream came tumbling down from the hill and flowed past a huge rock. The sound of the brook, as it murmured and gurgled on its way, floated up to him.

Pushing his bicycle towards the rock, the youth gestured towards him, indicating that he should follow. As he neared the rock, he observed it closely. The water was bright and clear, as though a young girl from the hills had come rushing headlong down the slope, chuckling happily to herself. The simile rose, unbidden, to his mind. These days, his mind searched for metaphors and similes whenever it was confronted with something that was unfettered and unimpeded. The youth stood on the rock, the bird. An often heard phrase came to his mind: 'free as a bird.' He was not very familiar with the world of nature. He could not identify the bird. Perhaps it was a kingfisher? It had a long beak, and a blue body. Perhaps there was fish in the stream. That was why the bird could not leave the place. It was bound by an invisible bond. As free as a bird!

The youth came splashing out from the water. The kingfisher suddenly took wing, frightened by the sound of footsteps. The youth put on his clothes again. Having wrung out the wet gamosa, he put it back into the bag. He slung the bag on his shoulder, and, looking at him, said, 'Come, let us leave. We must reach the village before it gets dark.'

Both of them climbed onto their bicycles again. He rode in front, the youth followed.

The hostage and his keeper. Both were now pedalling with the same idea in mind. A safe shelter from the soldiers and the security forces. It was as though he had arranged his own captivity. When news of the soldiers' approach reached them, he felt the same anxiety as the youth and those in the organization. And when they came to know that the soldiers had moved away, or when they reached a safe shelter, along with them, he, too, felt the same relief.

The narrow path became somewhat broader. This meant that their destination was not too far away now. He noticed bullock-cart tracks on the path. The youth's bicycle was now moving alongside his own. He looked at the youth. His face was calm and unconcerned. It was as though he was confident that there was now no possibility of either the security forces or the soldiers coming here. The unemotional state reflected in the youth's face spread to his own mind. Once more, his eyes strayed to the carelessly-slung bag on the youth's shoulder. The lethal weapon inside that bag was only fulfilling a formal purpose.

The weapon was no longer a harbinger of death. It was not just the sign of the relationship between the youth and himself: a symbol of authority. But was it only that?

He was a prisoner at one end of the metallic gun-barrel. But, at its other end, the youth, too, was a prisoner. He suddenly remembered the kingfisher, and the phrase came to his mind again. As free as a bird! But the bird was bound to the water in the stream by a strange relationship. He was a hostage; the youth was free. But the youth could not abandon him and go away. So the youth, too, was a prisoner. Until he himself was free, this youth would remain a captive. The power of this lifeless gun mutely controlled their relationship.

Abruptly, the youth halted. From beside a nearby tree, two other young men came towards them. He was a little taken aback. He had not realized that two people were standing nearby. The youth gestured that there was no need for alarm, which meant that the two others were also from the organization. They had a bicycle with them. His companion asked them something in the tribal tongue. He appeared to be satisfied with their reply. Once more, he climbed onto his bicycle and asked him to get up on his own bicycle again. The other two also climbed on theirs. All three bicycles now began to pick up speed.

It was almost dark when they reached the village that was their destination. He saw a bamboo platform beside the path leading into the village. Some young men were sitting on this bamboo platform. They had no lethal weapons in their hands. However, they had with them a couple of stout wooden sticks. A kerosene lamp was placed at a corner of the platform. Possibly these boys were there to guard the village. The youth who had accompanied him dismounted from his bicycle and talked to them in their own language. They all nodded and seemed to agree with him. Sitting on their bicycles again, the youth and he pedalled towards the village. The other two also moved along beside them.

It was a tribal village, in a remote area. Looking at the state of the huts, it was clear that there was a great deal of poverty here. The huts had roofs of thatch and bare walls of dry reed with slits between them. It was almost dark. The villagers were busy herding their cattle. The few people that they encountered showed no curiosity when they saw the strangers. Possibly the youth's organization often brought people to their village in this way.

Signs of extreme poverty were visible along the paths of the village as well. But it looked as though the same poverty had not yet managed to affect the healthy appearance of the few people whom he saw. And the signs of acute poverty were not quite as visible in the hut before which they eventually halted. Actually, it was not one, but two huts. A one-room hut stood beside the main one. Its sloping roof was made of thatch and its walls were attractively mud-plastered. The compound was clean, and a large storehouse was visible in a corner. There seemed to be a large plot of cultivated land behind the house. This plot was full of jackfruit and banana plants as well as areca-nut trees and betel creepers. A stout bamboo fence encircled the house, while a bamboo gate barred the entrance.

Looking at him, the youth said, 'We shall stay here tonight. This is the home of the village headman. Quite safe, in fact.'

The two others pushed aside the gate and, entering the compound, called out for the headman. However, the village elder had gone out and not yet returned. His son came out of the house instead and conducted them formally into the one-roomed house in the corner.

Inside was an armless, rough-hewn chair. He was asked to sit on it. On one side of the room was a low, wooden cot. Though the sheet that covered the bed was coarse, it was clean. The mild aroma of the plaster of dung and fresh earth was still in the room, which meant that the house had been cleaned not very long ago. The household had received news of their approach on this day itself. Of course, the decision to come here had been taken in haste. They usually shifted during the night. But only that morning they had come to know that a group of soldiers would reach their original hiding place that afternoon. That was why they had fled on their bicycles in broad daylight. The news of their approach here had been conveyed this morning through a messenger.

The headman's son brought a small bucket of water along with a brass jug and a clean gamosa, and requested him to wash his hands and feet. He was taken to a corner beside the house, which was enclosed by bamboo screens. A large slab of stone was laid out in this enclosed space, so that bits of earth would not spatter around. Because it was dark already, a kerosene lamp had been hung from the bamboo screen. Looking at the still un-dried bamboo of the screen, he realized that these arrangements had been made for his benefit. For them, he was a visitor. Did they know, he wondered, that he was a prisoner? How could they possibly imagine that this man, who seemed to move about so freely, was actually a captive?

After washing his hands and face, he felt quite refreshed. Wiping himself thoroughly with the gamosa, he entered the room once more. This, too, was illuminated by a lamp. The youth was waiting for him there. As soon as he entered, the youth got up from his chair. Even though nothing was said, he understood that there was respect in the gesture.

Instead of sitting on the chair, he went and sat on the bed. He said to the youth, 'Sit down.'

The reply came, 'You must be very tired today. Rest. We may have to stay here for a couple of days this time. Afterwards, we shall go to a safe camp in the hills. We shall have to cross dense jungles. It will be a difficult business. So rest here and regain your strength first.'

The youth took out two tablets from his pocket, and, offering them to him, said, 'Have these.'

He recognized them to be vitamin pills. He did not need vitamin pills for his health now, but along with the tablets, something else seemed to come to him. Was it the warmth in the youth's gesture? Or some kind of fellow-feeling? Another symbol of their relationship? He wanted to say something, but the youth went out to the veranda without waiting for his reply. He seemed satisfied with the silent communication between them.

As the youth left, he noticed that the bag was slung on his shoulder. It was his constant companion. The weapon gave notice of its identity from inside the bag. It was now an inert tube.

From the veranda, the youth shouted, 'I shall remain outside.'

But he knew that the youth would not remain outside. The words said to him, in a subtle language were, 'I have a duty. I shall perform that duty. But I also trust you. Don't escape from here and break that trust. My duty is inextricably linked to your cooperation.'

Strange, the power of these words! Even amidst the numerous opportunities for escape, these words had shackled him. But had these words conveyed the same meaning during the first few days of his captivity? Of course, during those first few days, they had had a powerful strength of a different kind. These words had then evoked mixed feelings of fear, agitation, helplessness and insecurity.

He heard the sound of footsteps outside. A middle-aged man came into the room. He understood that this was the head of the household. A small girl followed him in. In her hands was a platter of food. He caught the whiff of cooked chicken. The headman himself had brought a jug of water. With a great deal of care, the headman placed on the floor a mat that lay in a corner of the room. He put the jug beside it, while the little girl arranged the platter on it.

Formally and with humble gestures, the headman then asked him to come for his meal. He had brought a gamosa. This he placed on the mat. The headman said, 'There is little in our house to offer you. Please don't mind this simple food. The news that you would be coming reached us very late. It is my good fortune that a great leader such as you is staying in my house.'

From the headman's respectful words, it was apparent that the youth had explained his captive's identity in this manner. The headman told him to leave the platter outside the room after he had finished his meal. Turning up the lamp a little, the headman then left the room. He was extremely hungry. Even though the rice was parboiled, it tasted quite good when he mixed it with the chicken curry. Washing his hands and face on the platter itself, he took it and, opening the door, went out of the room. Sure enough, there were no guards outside. There was no way in which the door could be locked from the outside, either. Keeping the platter in a corner of the veranda, he re-entered the room and closed the door after him.

Sitting on the bed, he took out the notebook from the satchel that he carried with him. For the last three months or so, he had been keeping this journal of his captivity. The youth had brought him this notebook when he had expressed the desire to keep a journal. Out of his total captivity of seven months, he had kept a record of his daily experiences for the last three months. He had also written down, as far as he had been able, a record of the time before. Those entries, of course, were from memory.

As soon as he closed the door from inside, a sense of captivity engulfed him. Now it was as if he had willingly made himself captive. But even this self-imposed captivity felt normal for him. So long as the door had been open, he had not felt like this. The murmur of voices from the other house had created the impression of some link with it. That link was now severed. The room was lonely and silent. There was no opening now on any side. He felt at peace after imprisoning himself.

By not remaining there, the youth who had said, 'I shall remain outside,' had placed the prime responsibility for his own captivity on him. As long as the door was open, he had had a sense of unease. What if his mind hindered his feet from discharging that responsibility? What if his mind tempted his feet: 'The open sky is out there, there is freedom outside, go, get away!'

And what if his feet really went out through the door? What if they, his feet, refused to accept the bond of that unseen trust? But no, he had shut the door. He had accepted his captivity. He had accepted the discipline of the words, 'I shall remain outside.' And strangely, he felt at peace.

Rifling through the pages of the notebook, he glanced through the previous entries before writing down the experiences of that day. It had become a habit with him to read about the events of the past almost every day. In this manner, he wished to preserve intact the memories of these days.

He had written down the experiences of the first day on the very first page of the diary. On that day, they had put him inside a house and locked the door from outside. 'We shall be outside, don't try to escape.' How harsh, how frightening, the words had been that day! They had dragged him out from his own familiar world, and pushed him into another one. The memory of the moment made him shudder. That moment, when another vehicle had stopped before his own. Four gun-wielding youths had dragged him out from his car, and pushed him into the back-seat of another vehicle. That had been a terrifying moment. Later, however, he had realized that the logic of the youth's world was not the same as the logic of reason in his own ordered existence. He had heard them say several words which he himself used, or had read. However, since he could not understand the tribal language, those remained gestures for him. But even those gestures had had the power to create a sense of fear in him.

They also used some bookish English and Assamese words. Nation, state, revolution, imperialistic power, national consciousness, government, public, freedom, rights—in their world, the meanings of these words were completely different. The meaning of the word 'security' was also different in their world. This was because they had their own interpretation of the law. The entity that he had always thought of as a 'nation' was not, for them, a nation at all. They had created their own nation. In their eyes, his nation was an imperialist power. He had assumed that he was a citizen of a free country, but they said that he was the lackey of this imperialist power. Those laws which he had always thought of as a haven of security, were perceived by them to be the means of state terrorism. Their act of kidnapping was, for him, an act of terrorism; but they viewed it as their duty to their nation. The government which he thought provided them with social and political security was for them an illegitimate government. It was, for them, but a sand bar across the mouth of a river, to be swept away by the flood-waters of revolution. He had read of many revolutions. But with the barrels of their guns pointed at his body, these youths seemed to aim the revolution at him.

They had reassured him that he himself was quite insignificant. Their dissension was against the 'illegitimate imperialistic national power.' He had been taken hostage because he was a symbol of the repressive security arrangements of that government machinery. The national power accorded importance to symbols such as he, for that power was a repressive force. Repressive acts were carried out in the name of security. If the mask of security was lifted, that power would be revealed in its true self.

They had some demands to make of that machinery which called itself the government. (Some day, they would overthrow that power, but it would take time for the revolution to mature. Therefore, it was necessary for them to get the illegitimate government to accede to some of their demands in this way.) That other nation would grant them their demands, for it was to that imperialistic power's self-interest to have him freed. Because if he died, the mask of security which that power used as an excuse would be ripped apart.

However, they had not presented their reasoning in quite that manner. From what he could understand of their language when they talked with each other, he had inferred this logic. He got the impression that the ideas in the world that he lived in were controlled by a kind of linguistic centre. It was as though both groups of people, the youths' and his own, had what each one believed to be positive electromagnetic charges which, when they met, repelled each other. Even with his bureaucratic attitude (he was an important government officer) he could vaguely discern that both these worlds were deeply influenced by economic realities, and this had become intermingled with politics.

And he had been afraid. He could see no escape, no way out from the gulf between their world and his, or from the emptiness that enveloped him. For a long time, the meaning of their words, and their reasoning was hidden from him, like the words of a riddle. They did not inflict any physical torture on him at all. Though their manner of speaking was rough, they were not exactly disrespectful towards him. Once in a while, they also allowed him to exchange letters with those at home. But their way of thinking clashed repeatedly with his own. He had not been able to trust them. He would feel as though, at any moment, the muzzles of their guns would discharge their bullets into his breast.

But even greater than this physical fear had been the tremendous mental tension that he had felt. The physical hardships that he went through were of course quite considerable. Every day, they had to change shelters. He had no settled place to stay in. Nightly, they would wander through fields, wade through the chest-high water of rivers, march through dense jungles and marshes. Yet he would have shrugged off these physical hardships if he had only been able to trust them. Pushing him into various rooms at night, they would stand guard outside.

Occasionally, they would push him inside with the words, 'We shall remain outside. Don't try to escape.' Each word seemed weighted with ridicule, callousness, and cruelty. Each word seemed to express not just his own helplessness, but also that of the national power. As it wounded him, each word became synonymous with terror.

He had been unable to comprehend how a functionary could become the symbol of the government machinery. Yet they had assumed that by capturing him, they had unerringly dealt a devastating blow to the power of the government. They had thought that the bugle of revolution had been sounded loud and clear.

He had formed the impression that the youths were being guided by a grave error. And, like him, even the youths themselves did not understand what the outcome of that error would be.

He had not understood, either, whether the ideas in his mind were logical, or erroneous. But his mistrust of the youths had grown. This mistrust had also a simple reason behind it. His guards had been changed almost every week. By the time he came to know one group of youths who guarded him, they were changed. There was no conversation between him and them.

Only sometimes, when one or two of them who appeared to be some kind of leaders had come, only then had he the opportunity to talk. Looking at the unemotional faces of his guards, he had been unable to fathom their thoughts. He had been unable to trust them. Just as they assumed him to be the symbol of the government, he, too, had thought of each one of them as a diminutive symbol of terrorism.

But four months ago, everything had changed. The change had come from the very day that this youth had taken charge. Even within their own positive magnetic fields, they had discovered small negative charges. This had allowed their two minds to meet.

He did not know whether or not the youth was part of the higher echelons of power. But it was apparent that the youth was not just an ordinary guard. For, on many occasions, he took independent decisions without waiting for orders from above. The youth's pronunciation of English words had given him the impression that he was highly educated. Though tribal, he spoke Assamese fluently. They talked mostly of everyday matters. Sometimes, however, each of them expressed their opinions and talked of their ideals. The youth professed deep faith in their revolution, but would listen attentively to what he had to say. There was never any callousness or disregard in his words.

On the very first day that the youth had taken charge, he had made an arrangement that had changed the very nature of his captivity. Till then, the door had always been locked from outside after he had been put into a room. When the guards were nearby, they had trained their guns at him. The youth had had no gun in his hands on the first day when he had come to him. He had not brought along other guards, either. He had enquired into his wellbeing, and had also given him news of his family. As he was leaving, he had said, 'Latch the door from inside. I shall be outside. Don't be afraid.' He had gently shut the door behind him.

'Don't be afraid.' These words had a strange effect on him. The emptiness, the sense of discord that he had felt all these days, vanished in a moment. Because the words 'Don't be afraid' followed them, the meaning of the sentence 'I shall be outside,' too, had seemed to change. The difference between the two sentences, 'Don't try to escape' and 'Don't be afraid' represented two completely different ways of viewing the same situation.

However, the other circumstances remained unchanged. He had to be shifted frequently from one place to another. They had moved from village to village at night, stung by mosquitoes and bugs. There was no question of staying anywhere for any length of time. For the organization believed in always being in a state of extreme alertness.

The change was in his own mental condition. He was a hostage, the youth was his keeper. Yet, somehow, without their being aware of it, this relationship had now changed. In spite of the difference in their ages, there developed between them a bond of companionship. The youth had never behaved like a guard. Certainly, he always carried a gun in his bag. No doubt, the gun was the sign of their relationship, but that sign had undergone a basic change.

From a sign of terror, it had become a sign of trust.

And so while wandering on their journeys from village to village, through hills and valleys, sometimes he was the youth's teacher, while the youth was his disciple. Every now and again, the youth would mention some famous writer. At these times, the fact that he was very well-read had been a great help. He had been happy to be able to talk about those writers and their work.

The youth then listened to him like an attentive

student. But when the subjects were those relating to nature, rural life, agriculture, farming, and so on, the youth became the teacher, and he the student. He had no clear idea about the relationship between man and nature. In a strange way, this life of captivity helped him to augment the store of knowledge that he had had in his state of freedom.

After reaching a village, on one occasion, he had fallen seriously ill. The high fever made him pass out several times. Even in his semi-conscious state, he had been aware that the youth had secretly gone and fetched a doctor from a distant city. On becoming conscious, he had seen the youth sitting beside his bed. On his face there had been an expression of great anxiety. When the fever had finally subsided, he had come to know from the head of that household that the youth had not stirred from his side until he came round. The youth had given him his medicines, heated water for him; sponged down his body, put cold compresses on his forehead, and had even cleaned up his excrement, all in an astonishingly caring way. However, the youth had not expressed any emotion after he had recovered. He had merely said, 'Your family was not informed of your illness. They would have been worried. Hope you don't mind.' He had mumbled his gratitude.

After his fever had subsided, they had had to remain for quite some time in the same village till he had recovered his strength. During this period, the two of them had discussed a variety of topics. At that time, he had expressed a desire to keep a journal. He had thought that the youth would not agree to his keeping an account of his captivity. But he had readily agreed, and had brought him a notebook the very next day. After writing down his entries, he would always show them to the youth, who would read them. Sometimes, the youth would nod his head, as though he had been able to catch a glimpse of his soul through these entries. After his illness, he had felt a greater sense of uncertainty. His conscious mind had not been aware of this. But the youth, reading aloud from his journal, had pointed out to him how the uncertainty of his subconscious mind was revealed in these entries.

Once he had gained some strength, it was necessary for the youth to change their halting-places frequently. Sometimes, while pondering on the uncertainty of his ever being freed, he would become restless. This would be reflected in his journal.

One day, while reading these entries, the youth had said, 'You are impatient to be free, aren't you? But look, your government is not concerned about you at all. We have sent them some terms and conditions. We can release you as soon as those conditions are met.'

He had asked, 'And if they don't agree to your terms?'

On hearing his question, the youth was at a loss for words. After a while, he had said with a smile, 'In that case, you will have to become one of us. Would you mind?'

In the end, he had stopped thinking of freedom. He had accepted his captivity as the normal condition of his life now. Around this time, the youth had relaxed the vigilance that surrounded his captivity. After saying, 'I shall be outside,' the youth would go somewhere else instead of standing guard. From the very beginning, the youth had always carried his gun around unobtrusively, so that it had remained invisible to him. Sometimes, he would leave the bag containing the gun lying near him. It seemed as though without any outward sign, the youth was giving him numerous opportunities to escape. But on the other hand, even in the midst of these unlimited opportunities, they had been bound together with an invisible bond.

Around this time news that groups of soldiers, as well as the police, were searching these areas thoroughly for him had begun to trickle in. But he had not viewed these bits of information as something to be happy about. When news of the soldiers' approach would reach them, he, too, would become anxious. His mind would clamour to go with the youth to a place of 'safety'. A part of his conscious mind understood that this kind of behaviour would be considered illogical by everybody in his own world. Even then, whenever he heard of the approach of the soldiers seeking to free him, he would think of safety as a distance between those soldiers and himself. Safety, for him, was the gun in the youth's hands.

Today, when they received the news of the soldiers, they had immediately fled to the shelter of this village. After settling him down in this room, the youth had gone off somewhere else, perhaps to the main house, to sleep. And in the meantime, he had latched the door and accepted his captivity willingly.

As on other days, now, too, he wrote down the events of the day. Swallowing the two tablets that the youth had given him with a draught of water, he lay down on the rough bed. The safety of the bed seemed to embrace him.

He woke up at dawn to the sound of birdsong. Unlatching the door, he went out to the veranda. The head of the household was waiting for him to emerge from his room. With much ceremony, he brought a cane stool and, placing it on the veranda, requested him to sit on it. The little girl who had brought him his food the previous night, now brought him a bowl of black tea along with a little molasses. The others of the family appeared to be keeping a respectful distance from the 'leader.' Even though there was no milk in the tea he quite enjoyed sipping it from the bowl along with the molasses.

The two men who had brought them here the previous evening now appeared on the bicycle. They looked around for his guard. On hearing their voices, the youth came out from the other house. They informed him that this place was no longer safe. They had met some soldiers just a few kilometers away. The soldiers had stopped and searched them, and had asked them if they knew whether some strangers had come this way. They, however, had sent the soldiers in the direction of a distant village.

Listening to them, the youth said, 'We shall have to move camp today. These villages are not safe any more.'

For some time now, he had been on the verge of asking the youth a question. Because of a sense of hesitation in his mind, it remained unasked. But today, he abruptly questioned, 'What will you do if the soldiers surround the house and try to rescue me?'

His captor seemed unprepared for this sudden question. He did not answer immediately, but remained staring at him. After a while, the youth asked softly in return, 'Tell me, what will you do?'

This question in reply to his own startled him. He did not know what to reply.

The youth continued, 'If those circumstances arise, I shall have no choice but to execute you.'

On hearing this, he remained staring dazedly at the other man's face. This same person had nursed him devotedly to health through a serious illness, yet he was now talking quite unconcernedly of executing him!

The youth seemed to understand his feelings. He said, 'You are not our enemy. But don't have any illusions. A government seeks legitimacy by protecting its citizens. But we have to prove that your government cannot ensure the safety of its citizens. Your death will not be caused by me, or by our organization. Your government will be the cause of your death. If our revolution is to succeed, it will be my duty to kill you if those circumstances arise.'

Strange logic! He knew that no law of any country would ever accept this logic as just. But in the youth's world, it was this logic that had entrenched itself. He felt that his captors had no other alternative than to take this stand. The thought of his own execution caused an upheaval in his mind at first. But slowly it subsided. He felt quite calm. He seemed to leave his own sphere of logic and step into the youth's world. Even the words 'revolution', 'legality', 'justice' and so on acquired different meanings in this other world.

It was decided that they would begin their journey to the camp that very evening. In the meantime, the youth sent off some village lads to check the safety of the route along which they were to travel. One of these boys brought back devastating news while they were having their afternoon meal. The soldiers had searched out the camp, and destroyed it that morning. There was no question of going there now. Even though this hamlet was no longer as safe as it had been before, they would have to spend the night here. Tomorrow, they would move again in search of a place of safety.

The youth busied himself in strengthening the security arrangements for the night. Just before dusk, several new faces appeared. He got a hint of their weapons inside their bags. The youth who was his guard gave them many instructions. They went in different directions to watch the paths leading to the village. He also sent the headman and his family to another house for the night.

The youth said to him, 'We shall make special arrangements for this night. For your own safety, I shall have to spend the night in your room. Several of our Freedom Fighters will stand guard around the house. If we can see this night through, we can go to another place in the morning.'

From these words, he understood that the 'Freedom Fighters' had come to this village to secure his captivity.

They had their evening meal even before it grew dark. After a while, darkness engulfed the surroundings. The youth was with him in the dim lamplight of the room, standing, alert, beside the door. The silent, lonely surroundings seemed to throb. No one spoke. Today, the other man carried the lethal weapon in his hand openly. He himself remained sitting motionless on the bed.

Looking at him, the youth said, 'Go to sleep. I shall remain awake.'

But he remained sitting where he was. Even if he wished to sleep, would sleep come to him this night?

Perhaps he dozed. He woke up with a start when one of the guards outside banged the door and entered the room. This boy said something to the youth. He then went out again, shutting the door behind him.

The youth said, 'The enemy has surrounded us on all sides.' He looked at the youth. Their eyes met. The youth's gaze was steady and unblinking. He now gestured to him to leave he bed and come forward.

He heard some explosions outside. He realized that the sounds were not those of crackers. They were the sounds of gunfire. He got down from the bed and stood before the youth.

The youth trained the gun at his breast.

The final moment of his captivity had arrived. Could the final moment be as long as this!

Just then, he heard the sounds of several guns being fired at the same time. He thought, 'So this is what death is like.'

But why was he still conscious?

Everything seemed to happen at once. He saw great gobs of blood gushing out from the youth's mouth. His body was riddled with bullets. The gun slid from his hand, and his lifeless body crashed to the ground like a felled tree.

The final moment of his captivity had not turned into the moment of death. For the youth had not fired his gun. He had lowered it instead. And at that very moment, countless bullets crashed into the youth's body.

Several soldiers rushed into the room. One of them extended his hands towards him. He said, 'Captain Batra. Thank God! You are safe.'

Captain Batra had an RT set in his hands. The instrument crackled, Captain Batra spoke into it: 'Operation successful. Target safe. One terrorist killed.'

Terrorist! The word crashed against the magnetic centre in his skull, where it exploded loudly. Two words seemed to drag themselves agonizingly out from his mouth, 'Aaah, no!'

He sat beside the lifeless body of the youth. Placing his hand on his cold forehead, he remained staring at the open, lifeless eyes.

Captain Batra did not stop him. Standing beside the dead body, Captain Batra touched his cap with his hand in respect.

Moustache

Whenever the word moustache is mentioned, the picture that comes to my mind is that of Bhuri Mahajan's. A true idea of the colossal corpulence of the central portion of his body can only be found through the Bangla word bhuri: paunch, or embonpoint. My acquaintance with this word is not recent—I have known it since my youth. Those who spoke the same tongue as the Mahajan referred to him, in his absence, as Bhuri Mahajan, or Paunchy Merchant. His actual name had vanished completely from public memory.

Next to his mansion, which was as huge as a dinosaur, was our puny little house. We would often look at him with envy. Indeed, there was no way we could avoid looking at him, for at a particular time every day, he would be visible for a while in the vast veranda of the mansion. At one end of the veranda was an ordinary string cot. On this unsightly cot, at exactly the same time every day, he would repose his even more unsightly and spherical belly.

My abhorrence for moustaches arose from the

strangely-shaped moustache of this Bhuri Mahajan. At that time, the first signs of my impending manhood were declaring themselves. On my upper lip was a fuzzy suggestion of a moustache. Suddenly, the reason why this forty-plus, middle-aged Bhuri Mahajan always sat on the cot on his veranda at a particular time every day had dawned on me. Giving up the rolls of fat on his body to be massaged by the expert hands of an ugly flunkey, at exactly ten in the morning, Bhuri Mahajan would gawk with a hungry stare at the movements of the people on the road. A flourishing salt-and-pepper moustache topped his thick, dark lips. This growth of hair came flowing down the sides and concealed his greedy mouth. Without his being aware of it, his tongue would keep licking it. It would seem as though the sap of lust, secreted by his tongue, dribbled down from the corners of his mouth.

I discovered its nature through certain actions within my own rebellious body. At that same time every day, some unknown attraction would make me, too, come out and stand on the veranda of our house. There was a hostel of a girls' school near our house, and the real reason for that attraction lay in the rhythmic swaying of the blossoming bodies of the girls. Since I had a feeling of guilt in my mind, and since my elders looked at me as a harmless boy, for after all they could not divine the extreme restlessness of the blood in my veins, I had to be careful about watching this daily blissful performance. I found the appearance of Bhuri Mahajan at that time everyday quite intolerable. I felt that if Bhuri Mahajan came to know of this secret conduct of mine, so would everybody else. I would become quite disturbed at this prospect. When the swaying bodies of the young girls drew me to the veranda of our house, I would see, on his string cot, Bhuri's bloated, revolting condition. I would look sideways at him with a terrible feeling of guilt. I would be afraid that Bhuri would divine the actual intent of my naked mind.

It was in such circumstances that one day I chanced upon Bhuri's ugly nature. I saw Bhuri's restless, greedy eyes travel thirstily and restlessly over the swaying bodies of those girls. I could not see his mouth, which, along with the sides of his chin, was covered with that vast moustache. But it seemed as though, hiding behind his moustache, countless lustful tongues were licking the edges of his mouth, and gratifying themselves. A feeling of disgust grew in my mind. It seemed as though by offering his corpulent frame up to the strong hands of his devoted flunkey to be ravished through massage, Bhuri was controlling his own feelings of dissatisfaction. It seemed to me as though his moustache was a disguise, behind which the spittle drooled freely down the sides of his mouth.

My revulsion for moustaches was born at that time. Whenever I think of a moustache, the image of Bhuri's lustful face and his drooling mouth, camouflaged by his moustache, comes before my mind. Therefore, that facial hair, the moustache that bestows a young lad with the joy of manhood, became, for me, the cause of distress. Barely had I reached the first year in college, when I sacrificed my moustache. Later, even though my acute hatred for moustaches dimmed somewhat, I did not feel it necessary to acquire one, at least till I left college.

All of us assembled at the parade ground. We were all from different places, having left behind different kinds of lives. There were college lecturers, schoolteachers, trainees or junior employees of some industrial house, and bank employees. But there was a feeling of satisfaction within us—we had successfully cleared a competitive examination to climb this rung on the ladder of success. A slight arrogance had built up in our minds. Even though we were young, we had, in the meantime, entered our various spheres, and were under the impression that we had adopted the grave demeanour of older people.

But as soon as we announced our arrival at the training centre, a huge battle was waged with razors on our carefully tended hair. This was the first assault on our individuality. In addition, we were made to wear a pair of baggy khaki shorts. Thus revealed, our hairy legs were the cause of acute discomfort to us. This was the second blow to our self-esteem. In our short, wide half pants, with our clipped hair, each one of us regressed to a kind of mature childhood. Our strange appearance seemed to bring with it a kind of youthful restiveness. In the eyes of our teachers, whom we referred to as 'Ustads', we seemed to have been transformed into immature students.

On the very first day, they made us run around the parade ground till we were short of breath. If somebody sat down in exhaustion, they pulled him up and, shoving him into the group again, made him run around once more. Our tears and sweat mingled freely, amidst the encouraging shouts and pushes of the Ustads. Finally, when we reached our places again, we pleaded in a single voice: Ustad, we cannot take it any more, let us off for today. At this, smiles of delight appeared on the faces of the Ustads. They said, rest for five minutes. We leaped up, shouting with joy, and rushed off in the direction of the shade of a huge banyan tree in a corner of the field.

A colossal sound, like a clap of thunder, was heard then, and rooted our feet to the ground. We heard that command, 'Jaise the, as you were!' The source of that command: a grave face, a muscular, powerful body, belonging, as we came to know later, to our Chief Physical Training Instructor. The way he looked at our slack bodies, it seemed as though that belittling gaze told us that we were, each one of us, insignificant and lowly beings.

That glance was a tremendous slap to our pride. From the cavern of his mouth began to emerge in sequence some words, which defined us on that parade ground. We thought that after clearing the competitive examinations, each one of us was now a very important officer. But thanks to the words from his dictionary unleashed on us by our Chief Instructor, we learned that one of us was a sissy, another a pregnant cow, yet another a clod, somebody else a miserable specimen of humanity.

Much, much later, we came to know that the reason behind this deliberate shattering of our egos and individualities was to rebuild it once more, and to bring a sense of balance to our minds and bodies. Only then were we able to gaze at our shapely, growing muscles with a sense of pride. But that came later, much later.

A huge amount of suffering had already begun on the parade ground. The tremendous pressure of discipline made us see stars. Every limb was captioned by the adjectives issuing from the Chief Instructor's mouth. Instead of mending our broken individuality, the sympathetic and encouraging words of the Ustads seemed to oppress us even more. When the time allotted to physical training came to a close, we would anoint our painful limbs with soothing unguents, and try to brace ourselves. Every day, we noticed that the level would be raised. We would be ashamed of our clumsy bodies. We were reaping the fruits of neglecting to exercise during our youth and childhood.

It was not as though all of us were in the same boat. We, in other words, the trainees, were divided into different squads. The physical limitations were more apparent in our squad. This was because most of the members of our squad came from a background where book learning was given more importance than physical exercise and fitness.

But as the days went by, our growing suppleness began to fill us with amazement. We began to notice that the muscles were becoming stronger. The fat that had slyly collected in various parts of our bodies disappeared.

Even though we could not approach the level that had been set by the Chief Instructor, we moved up several rungs in the ladder of physical fitness.

However, it was not as though all of us moved ahead at the same levels of improvement. Vijay Raman, from our squad, lagged pitiably behind on the parade ground. Unable to balance his body to the commands 'Right Turn', 'Left Turn', 'About Turn' and so on, the intelligent young man who had graduated with ninety per cent marks, became an object of derision. He became the prime target of the Chief Instructor's sarcasm and began to be adorned with ever-newer adjectives.

It was not as though Vijay Raman shirked his work during training. There was no letup in his efforts. Yet every day, he would commit some ludicrous blunder. The rest of us were all fond of Vijay, for he was a very quiet person who extended his friendship to one and all. He was also generous. As we observed his daily humiliations, sympathy arose in our minds. We tried to help him out in many different ways. But the determined efforts he made to improve his body kept us back from expressing our sympathies.

After a few months, we suddenly realized that a change had come over Vijay. Suddenly, his tottering steps firmed up. He was able to obey the commands of the Ustads quickly and correctly. His personality underwent an amazing change. From the mouth of the very same instructor whose arrows of ridicule would previously wound him, he now began to hear a few words of praise.

(It may be mentioned here that by then, a few words of praise had begun to come our way, as well.) Observing the change in him, the Ustads began to buoy him up with encouraging words such as 'Shabash!'

Even after all these days, the rest of us had not been able to conquer our sense of inferiority in spite of our heroic efforts to do so. How had this change in Vijay become possible? Had he won the mental battle against the Chief Instructor by taking refuge in some strategy, some tactic? We investigated the matter. A creative person among us discovered that Vijay's hour of triumph had coincided with the appearance of a luxuriant moustache on his upper lip. All of us realized that though Vijay had not sported a moustache previously, for some days now a moustache had begun to enhance the beauty of his face. The two tips of this flourishing growth were gradually beginning to point upwards. The more the moustache began to resemble a pair of horns, side by side, the power of his personality, too, began to increase. We did not know what kind of psychological relationship there existed between a pair of moustaches and the owner's personality. A few among us who were his well-wishers, thought that it would be best to ask him openly about this strategy of his.

On hearing our query, he laughed uproariously—again, a new aspect of his changed personality. He pointed out Santaan Sarma, of another squad. We used to call Santaan Sarma 'Horse', for out of all the trainees, he was the most fleet-footed. He was an exhibitionist as well, in the sense that he loved to show off his skill and expertise. Undoubtedly, he was the best among us all. He was restless and skilled. His limbs were well-knit and firm, while on his face was a rough harshness. When Vijay pointed him out, we immediately noticed his horn-like moustaches, whose two ends proudly pointed upwards in a bow-like arc in an explosion from two sides of his nose. While eating, sleeping, or exercising, this pair of moustaches had constantly caught our eye earlier, as well. But till then, we had not paid it much attention. In other words, till Vijay pointed it out to us, we had not been attracted by the special traits of this moustache. The overall coarseness of his rough face eclipsed the grand moustache. It was as though the moustache was not an independent entity, but an indivisible part of his entire body. It was for this reason that we had failed to notice its special trait. We realized that if Santaan Sarma's moustache were to be chopped off, his personality would disappear.

Vijay told us that when his self-loathing had reached its peak, when even after much effort, he had been unable to master the art of the parade ground, when he had even been thinking of calling it a day, the picture of Santaan Sarma's uncouth personality had come to his mind. He thought that if he began preparations afresh, with Santaan Sarma's personality as an ideal model, perhaps he could succeed.

Vijay could not easily imitate Santaan Sarma's behaviour, but he could take as his inspiration a symbol that would always guide and illuminate him, and subduing his self-loathing, develop his mind and body in the proper manner. At that moment, his eyes fell on Santaan Sarma's stunning moustache. He immediately decided to grow one himself. As soon as the moustache on his upper lip began to sprout, and then flourish, he began to get inspired. The shameful helplessness of his body ended.

We were in raptures on hearing about the inspirational role of his moustache in the improvement of Vijay Raman's mind and body. We began to accord the moustache a certain respect. Each one of us began to sport a uniquely patterned moustache. This all-pervading proliferation of moustaches must have come to the notice of the Ustads, for we came to know that they referred to us as the 'Moustachioed Group'.

I, too, grew a moustache. After sacrificing my moustache when I had become peeved with Bhuri Mahajan, this was the first time that any kind of facial hair on my upper lip adorned my visage. Perhaps unconsciously, I replicated Santaan Sarma's moustache pretty exactly over my own mouth. Indeed, Vijay Raman once said, 'Bhai, with that moustache of yours, you might be mistaken for Santaan Sarma's duplicate.' I changed the pattern of my moustache then.

For what I wanted was Santaan Sarma's powerful personality. I had no wish to be known as his duplicate, or clone.

In due course, we left the training centre, and took up our responsibilities in different areas of the country. Even though we did not meet, we kept in touch with what was happening in each others' lives. Somebody would begin to grow a moustache, and tend it in newer styles, newer modes. Others would bid goodbye to their facial fuzz. I myself stopped imbuing my moustache with any special significance, but on the other hand, I did not feel the necessity of removing it, either.

Even though Santaan Sarma's field of work and mine were different, we kept hearing of each other, for our places of work were near each other. Towards the end of our training period, a friendship had sprung up between us. We kept in touch through letters.

Through our work, we came face to face with a variety of experiences. We faced difficult problems. If we were able to solve them, we experienced the joy of success. From the head of our division, I came to know of Santaan Sarma's various triumphs. He had fired on a procession in order to break it up. My superior, Rao Saheb, kept a tab on all the details of what was going on in the division. I came to know through him that if that procession had not been broken up in that way, there would have been a serious law and order problem. This was the official version.

The newspaper headlines highlighted another outlook, another point of view. Pictures of those who had died and been wounded in the firing appeared. Strong protests began to spread against the incident, and a cartoon of Santaan Sarma appeared, in which he was captioned, 'The Sultan of Terror'. No doubt his likeness in the cartoon was a lampoon and a caricature, but I noticed that his vast moustache was depicted without any distortion at all. He held a humungous imaginary weapon of destruction that was even bigger than the hand that held it.

Santaan became a sultan. The cartoons made the most of the opportunity to play with his strange name. His parents had lovingly named him Santaan, or child. They had had no progeny for a long time. They had been almost middle aged, when, according to him, he had made his appearance in this world, vehemently protesting as he had done so. Unable, in their boundless adoration to find a suitable name for him, his parents had finally named him Santaan. He had told us in jest that because he had had to enter this world kicking and screaming in protest, a kind of resentment against the world had remained within him.

I began to hear many stories concerning Santaan Sarma, from various sources. He continued to hog the headlines. From official sources, I heard of his successes too. Opinions varied about his exploits: some called them feats, others said they were faults.

But as we became totally bound up in our work, gradually, the exchange of letters between Santaan and me dwindled, and then stopped altogether. But it could not be said that our friendship waned because of this. Therefore, when his name blared forth from the headlines once more, I felt it necessary to give him some advice. The incident involved a fierce lathi charge against an enraged group of ladies. The press splashed pictures of a nameless lady who had fallen victim to the blows of the police lathis, her clothes in such disarray that she appeared semi clothed. In the cartoons, Santaan Sarma was now re-christened with appellations such as Shaitan Singh, and so on. I wrote him a letter, asking him to exercise some control.

He replied immediately. He wrote that his department had entrusted him with certain responsibilities. They had also given him certain powers. Those powers were concentrated on his lathi. Therefore, if in the pursuit of his duties, the necessity for using the lathi arose, he would not hesitate to do so. I had perhaps written something about a sense of values in my letter. Dismissing my views, he wrote back saying that values were not rooted, or fixed immovably in people. A person's values were shaped by his environment, his field of work. It could not be helped if a difference in the way of looking at life, or a different point of view, brought along with it a difference in values, as well.

I did not fully comprehend his philosophy and I did not write to him again.

Suddenly, however, I received a letter one day. It was after a long time that I was getting a letter from Santaan Sarma. Even though we had not communicated for a quite a while, the cordiality that I felt for him had remained intact, in spite of the many controversial things that I read about him in the papers.

He wrote, 'I'm facing a terrible problem. You have to come…it is absolutely urgent.'

That was all. There was no preface, no explanation,

nothing. But since Santaan Sarma had written to me in this manner, the problem had to be critical indeed. The local papers had been silent about Santaan Sarma's exploits for some time, for he had been transferred to a distant place. Even if there were something to write about, the news would appear in the local papers of his area.

Taking leave of absence from my job for several days, I packed and went to him. On reaching, I saw that Santaan was not overly worried. His harsh face, firm chin, well-tended moustache were all adorning his powerful personality, as before. I met Vijay Raman, as well as several of our friends from the days of the Training College. Santaan informed us that all these friends had been summoned because there was some brainwork needed. It was necessary to have a strategic session. A local paper had charged him with rape.

Opening the paper, he showed us the report. I realized that there was an extremely serious allegation against Santaan Sarma. While on a raid, he had committed heinously oppressive acts against small children in an indescribably cruel manner. Beating the seriousness of even that was the allegation of rape committed on a sixteen-year-old girl. I quaked inwardly. Looking at the others, I realized that they too were very disturbed. However, Santaan himself did not appear to be at all bothered. He informed us that he was no rapist. This was the creation of an ugly and warped mind. He was no coward, he said, and he could very well tackle the situation himself. But there was a writ in the High Court, and the High Court had ordered a Test Identification Parade, or TIP. He had asked permission from his department for a Revision Petition, but his present boss was of the opinion that it was better that he should clear the TIP. A revision would only serve to increase suspicions.

Santaan Sarma told us that he would stand in the TIP. But he suspected that there was some kind of conspiracy being plotted against him. Thanks to the papers that were against him, the general public was familiar with his appearance. Somebody could quite easily point him out deliberately. This was why it was necessary to think up a strategy to counter this conspiracy. Our help was needed in this.

The rest of us looked at each other. It would be truly appalling if somebody had really conspired to implicate Santaan Sarma in a false scandal. We, too, could not escape being spattered with some of that ignominy for we belonged to the same government service. We decided that we had to save Santaan from this terrible conspiracy. But how?

My eyes went to Vijay Raman's face. I noticed that his moustache had become even thicker. Santaan Sarma's moustaches had been the inspiration for that moustache. Looking at Santaan's moustache, I saw that his haughty moustache was arrogantly pointing heavenwards from the two verandas of his cheeks. I realized that it was this moustache that would endanger him at the TIP. In the paper that he had given us to read I had seen long descriptions of his moustache, dripping with derision, scorn, ridicule and harsh criticism. We decided that this moustache, which posed a danger to us, would itself become a weapon of salvation.

Each one of us who had assembled there as Santaan's friends had a carefully cultivated moustache. Since there were still quite a few days left for the TIP, we came to the decision that each one of us would grow our facial hair in the pattern of Santaan Sarma's moustache, and join in the TIP.

All seven of us friends took part in the TIP in this way. We saw that in the meantime, Santaan Sarma had changed the design of his moustache. The ends, which had arched heavenwards, now pointed to the ground. Flowing down the sides of his chin, its changed shape altered his appearance. This new shape reminded me of the moustache of Bhuri Mahajan of my youth. Seeing the altered shape of Santaan's moustache, I was a little annoyed as well, for according to the strategy we had worked out, it had been agreed that all of us were to stand at the TIP with similar moustaches.

The TIP began. A meek, rustic-looking, sixteen-year-old girl with drooping head looked at our faces with a dazed and fearful gaze, and moved on. She stared at our moustaches with amazement. But she was unable to point anybody out. She left the room after the TIP, and we came out with the joy of success writ large on our faces. While leaving the room, we were fleetingly aware of a middle-aged man standing near the girl. He looked intently at our faces as each one of us passed him.

That evening, we welcomed our success with great feasting and wining and dining at a joyful celebration in Santaan's house. It was almost midnight when I returned from the party to the Circuit House. As I was about to enter my room, I noticed a man waiting in a corner of the veranda.

Seeing me, he came up. Looking at me, he said, 'My daughter is ruined. She is totally destroyed…' I realized that this was the middle-aged man whom we had seen during the TIP.

He was the father of the girl.

I was a little irritated. 'The TIP is over. Your daughter could not identify anybody. Why have you come here now? What are you looking for?'

The man replied, 'Yes, my daughter could not identify anybody. How was I to know that she would fail to do so? Such huge moustaches! But I have recognized, I have definitely recognized. My daughter—in front of my very eyes…' the rest of the man's words were choked in a sob.

I grew impatient. I said, 'Your daughter could not identify anybody. The game is up now. Your plot has been exposed. Go away, don't bother me, it's midnight.'

The man, too, seemed to become angry at this point. He straightened up and stood erect. The rage that had collected in his face threatened to come bursting out. His voice came out in a shrill scream, 'The game is not up yet. Just because you say so, it's not all over yet. I myself shall do the identification. I shall certainly identify… it was dark that night. But what if it was dark? By the brightness of the lightning I could see quite clearly. Will I ever be able to forget this monstrous moustache? I have recognized it. These moustaches...I cannot be fooled. I shall certainly identify...yes, I shall certainly identify you.'

I felt as though I had been struck by a shaft of lightning. What was this man saying? He was going to identify me?

Santaan Sarma's face came to my mind. In a flash, the reason behind the change in pattern of Santaan's moustache became clear. Certainly, Santaan's war strategy had been successful. This man was under the impression that I was Santaan.

I stood rooted to the spot. How could I tell the man that I was not connected with the rape? By joining in the TIP, I had taken on a moral responsibility. Weighed down with shame, remorse and guilt, my arrogant moustache drooped down the sides of my chin.

Yawn

For a long time, Jeevan Krishna had not had much interest in nature. For this reason, he did not easily notice the weather, or the change of seasons. His mind became lively only wherever there was any human activity. It was social contact that was important to him.

The morning was clear, with fair weather. A bright ray of sunshine, too, had entered through a gap in the curtains of the window, and was dancing merrily in a corner. As he awoke, his mind merely slid over this sight. Even in the midst of this unconnectedness, however, there was clarity in his mind. For he remembered that this was a special day. He had concocted an important stratagem and he had no doubt that it would result in good fortune for him.

Doctor Haren had been sent with a message to the Korta. He was supposed to return with the Korta's statement of blessings. The Korta was now in exile, far away from active politics. Indeed, even the faculty of speech had abandoned him. Yet even now, he had an amazing hold over the party. Not everybody understood his sign language but Doctor Haren, besides being a good medical practitioner, was also recognized to be the acknowledged interpreter of the Korta's gestures.

Jeevan Krishna did not doubt that behind the seemingly unanimous acceptance of the Korta's leadership was an active discord within the party. The Korta's authority was boundless, for he was situated above all factional discord, and this was the reason why his divine pronouncements were necessary at the end of each inter-faction squabble. The Korta's disinterest in the current political situation from his place of exile, and his complete lack of desire for leadership strengthened his unwritten authority.

Whenever there was infighting within the party, whenever, to the delight of the Opposition, there was the danger of a split, it was always vital to seek the wise counsel of the Korta. Every faction would go running to the Korta in search of a solution to each and every danger. The disunity within the party had nourished his authority, his voiceless immobility and the apparent distance to his present dwelling created an aura about him. The inaccessibility had provided fodder for many fables about him, and had metamorphosed him into a mythical figure. Even after the Korta's speech was stilled, for a time, he would write down his advice by hand. But after paralysis struck the Korta's right arm and leg, he had had to create a new language through facial expressions, signs, and gestures. Doctor Haren's role had increased in importance after this. Not only was he the Leader's doctor, since he was also deeply acquainted with the Korta's mental world, it was he who could correctly interpret the true meaning of the signals.

There was a second reason for Doctor Haren's pronouncements being universally accepted within the party. Even though he was in close proximity to politicians, the doctor was himself quite apolitical. Yet not only did he have a well-informed finger on the pulse of the leaders of the party, he also had an understanding of the inner workings of the cadres within the party. The doctor commanded the trust of every faction.

At the time when the Korta, of his own free will, went into exile, Jeevan Krishna was a rising star in the party. Of course, he was still midway up the hierarchy of leadership. The Korta had had unbridled power within the party at that time. Therefore, like everybody else, Jeevan Krishna, too, had been amazed at the Korta's decision, but had thought that it had been caused by a dwindling interest in power. Like everybody else, this voluntary sacrifice of power by the Korta turned the respect that Jeevan Krishna felt for him to veneration.

In the meantime, Jeevan Krishna's political experience matured. His own impression was that he had acquired skill and dexterity in the sphere of diplomacy and its subtleties. He realized that unbridled power actually diminishes that power, and also that if there is power, there is also withdrawal of power. Jeevan Krishna began to think that exile was a remarkable ploy of the Leader's, arising from the wisdom garnered through his political acumen. This ploy bequeathed a divine authority above and beyond the limits of power, where there was limitless authority but no conflict of power, where the unvoiced expressions on the face of the Leader were themselves a form of control. After understanding this, Jeevan Krishna's veneration had lessened, but his respect for the Korta's political acumen had only increased.

Jeevan Krishna was now the leader of a strong faction within the party, and himself a cause for factional disaffection. This was because he was one of the candidates for the leadership of the party. He realized that in this battle for power, his challenger could only be the present leader of the party. The Korta's position was far above them. Jeevan Krishna believed that the time had now come to use, for his own gains, the same knowledge which the Korta had used to rise to a position of authority.

To put it simply, Jeevan Krishna wanted the party leadership. And without the Korta's blessings, he could not wrest that position. For a long time, all the decisions of the party needed the sanction of the Korta's blessings.

Jeevan Krishna had realized that the Korta believed firmly that the non-verbal indications he gave were completely intelligible to his interpreter, Doctor Haren. The Korta had absolute faith in the integrity of the doctor in interpreting that non-verbal language, and relaying them to others. In addition, the doctor was the only interpreter of that language. Jeevan Krishna's gameplan to wrest power was based on this strategy of the Korta's, and on Doctor Haren's interpretations.

It is always necessary to have minor schemes to back up any major stratagem. For quite a while, Jeevan Krishna had been employing such ploys. Open rebellion against those in power did not form any part of these strategies. Jeevan Krishna was a firm believer in nourishing his own clout in the shade of the power of others, and had climbed the ladder of successive stages of leadership in this manner. He had reached his present position through being acknowledged as a supporter of the present party leader. He had carefully and secretly nurtured a faction, as well.

Jeevan Krishna believed in the politics of opportunity, and recently, he had got on the track of just the kind of opportunity he had been looking out for.

This quest had been brought to him by the doctor. Doctor Haren was apolitical, or, in other words, a person with no political aspirations. But because of his long association with it, he was also a well-wisher of the party. Every ambitious person within it believed that Doctor Haren was his well-wisher solely. Because of this, nobody hesitated to voice his own secret aspirations before the doctor. Besides, his role as the analyzer and interpreter of the Korta's sign language, was also very important. This Doctor Haren had become part and parcel of Jeevan Krishna's plot.

At present, there was a battle in progress within the party between principles and morality. In fact, it could be said that a yawning chasm of difference of opinion had come into being between the personal morals of the ambitious and rising members of the party, such as Jeevan Krishna himself, and the party leader's political principles. Recently, the party leader had ruled that each and every office bearer should declare all their movable and immovable assets. In addition, they had been told that a neutral examiner would scrutinize those declarations.

At first, Jeevan Krishna had been quite pleased. For Jeevan Krishan had been under the impression that this edict was not applicable to the leader's faithful supporters, and that the main target of this infallible weapon was Nayak Dangoriya, the ringleader of another faction. The banner of open rebellion that Nayak had defiantly planted was becoming uncomfortable for the leader. But these days, the leader was beginning to give unnecessary and undue importance to morality. He had given strict orders that even trusted supporters such as Jeevan Krishna had to submit their list of assets. He became panicky. The leader wanted a coming together of principles and morality.

Jeevan Krishna believed that presence of mind, and a fruitful quest for opportunity were of greatest importance within the party. He did not believe that the means employed to achieve an end had to be, in themselves, impeccable. He had assumed that this new stand regarding the compatibility of principles and morality was a result of some kind of senile dementia. But the opinions, fraught with significance, that Doctor Haren gave when he came to treat the carbuncle in his thigh left Jeevan Krishna in no doubt whatsoever that this was an extremely subtle tactic of the leader.

The interview between Jeevan Krishna and Doctor Haren can be reconstructed in this manner:

Doctor Haren: (applying force on Jeevan Krishna's carbuncle) Eess, eess, the carbuncle has become really huge. But don't worry, I'll drain out the pus and put a dressing on it, it will heal up quite nicely. (Squeezing the carbuncle) Is it painful? Just a little bit more, it's almost done…

Jeevan Krishna: (contorting his face in agony) Uh. Aaah! Uhu, Hu, Uhu…!

Doctor Haren: (applying more force, and cleaning up the pus with cotton wool) You'll feel better once the pus is out. With this type of carbuncle, unless the germs are taken out completely… (looking at Jeevan Krishna's agonized face) There, that's done. Are you feeling a bit better? That's it, just change the dressing daily for a few days. Make sure it doesn't get infected. (Washing his hands with soap.) But is there some kind of carbuncle-sharbuncle within your party, as well? The Party Leader has used a very strong antibiotic, hasn't he?

Jeevan Krishna: (relieved from the pain of the carbuncle, but inwardly startled at the doctor's last words) Eh, I wonder what kind of medicine you're referring to?

Doctor Haren: This dose that he's administered. It seems that both the Faction That Digs and the Faction That Barks got the same medicine. Even though the target appears to be Nayak Dangoriya, the real target is somebody else. It seems the real virus is to be found in the ranks of the so-called supporters. That germ needs to be finished off. Nayak Dongoriya is of the Faction that Barks, while those who practice underhand ploys form the Faction that Digs. This is the way to vanquish both of them.

Jeevan Krishna: (experiencing a piercing feeling in his heart, the titter that issues from his mouth in order to cover his doubt and confusion is as unnatural as an inexperienced actor's. The vision of the three skyscrapers and a commercial concern he owns, incognito, floats before his eyes) Heh heh, the leader has, after all, every right to ask for the list of assets. I fully support his principles. Uuh! (his carbuncle grazes the chair that he is sitting on.)

Doctor Haren: Did you hurt the sore against something? (checks the dressing) No, it's all right. Be careful about sitting and getting up for a few days. (changing the subject) So, what were we talking about? Ah yes. Of course, nobody should object to the Party Leader asking for property ownership lists. But there is bedlam in the party. Everybody says that this is the time to strengthen the grassroots organization of the party. Just like what you've been doing. Who, after all, is the person who has brought in so many senior members into the party?

Jeevan Krishna: (doubting the meaning of the doctor's words, and looking at his face) Has the Korta said anything to you about this? (getting new members is

Jeevan Krishna's strategy for increasing the strength of his own faction)

Doctor Haren: No, he hasn't said anything. It's I who have been thinking along these lines, after seeing your organizational capacity. But it seems you too have received a notice asking for a full list of your assets? The Party Leader should not have been so inflexible. You are after all his trusted supporter. (Jeevan Krishna sees an expression of sympathy on the doctor's face. The conversation continues...)

It was not as though this conversation only opened Jeevan Krishna's eyes. Doctor Haren, too, grew closer to him after becoming a party to his secrets. No doubt Jeevan Krishna was in a bit of a flap after getting to know the actual significance of the strategy. But he himself had reached this peak of success only after becoming an expert in the subtleties of divisive politics. It was Jeevan Krishna's belief that any strategy could be countered by another ploy—what was needed was just diplomatic skill. If the leader was wily, Jeevan Krishna was wilier. The leader had once been a pugilist, and he had now demonstrated a wrestler's grip. But Jeevan Krishna too was quite adept at using contortions and grasps in politics. It was not just necessary to loosen the leader's grip with another; he would need to be totally floored, as well. For this, it would be necessary for Jeevan Krishna to revolt openly, but behind this revolt, there would be a secret stratagem.

Jeevan Krishna's self-confidence had increased of late. Many of the new members were his well-wishers, and he knew how to put them to 'good use'. Keeping this purpose in mind, the farsighted Jeevan Krishna had arranged to put certain handpicked members in some minor posts. Even though these posts were small, they were important, for it was the people in these posts who controlled the ordinary members. These people would be his pawns and foot soldiers.

But the role of these pawns and foot soldiers would be confined to the exterior battle. Inside, a secret plan for another battle was being drawn up. Jeevan Krishna had no faith in Nayak Dangoriya. In fact, as far as the future leadership of the party was concerned, Jeevan Krishna considered Nayak Dangoriya to be his chief competitor and prime opponent. But politics breeds strange bedfellows, and opportunism makes momentary friends of even sworn enemies. For this reason, it did not take very long for Jeevan Krishna to come to an understanding with Nayak Dangoriya. The secret plot that they planned was for the removal of the leader from his position. His place would be usurped by Nayak Dangoriya. Both of them headed two large factions within the party. Helped by the active members of both factions, both heads were now strongly placed at the grassroots level of the party. In contrast, however, the leader's neurotic behaviour made him appear to be out of touch with reality. His connection with the grassroots cadres, too, was tenuous. Both Jeevan Krishna and Nayak

Dangoriya possessed the asset of a gift of oratory. With this eloquence, they would inspire the grassroots cadres, whose demands for a change of leadership would resound all around.

This offensive would be the countergrip that would render useless the clench used by the ex-pugilist leader. But under the surface of this visible ploy was another, secret stratagem, concocted by Jeevan Krishna. He did not have the slightest desire to install Nayak Dangoriya in a position of leadership. The opportunist knows exactly when to make the best use of opportunity. This was a golden opportunity for Jeevan Krishna to take up the reins of leadership in his own hands. It would be Jeevan Krishna, and not Nayak Dangoriya, who would take the leader's place. Not only would the strategy be used to topple the leader, but also put Nayak Dangoriya out of action.

Jeevan Krishna believed Nayak Dangoriya to be a man of dull intellect, He had greater faith in his own Krishna-like wily cleverness than in the Balaram-type warlike postures of Nayak Dangoriya. In addition, Jeevan Krishna believed that the stars of his horoscope were always in a kind configuration favourable to him. Things would not be any different this time.

Otherwise, the active support of an apolitical person like Doctor Haren, who was so faithful to the Korta, would not have come to him so unexpectedly.

Jeevan Krishna's plan had the following phases.

1. Nayak Dangoriya and Jeevan Krishna would

activate the followers of both their factions, and openly spread various accusations against the present leadership among them.

2. The compelling demands for a change in the leadership of the party would unite the two factions.

3. There would be a demand for a meeting of the Central Committee, and if the leader did not agree to that demand, Jeevan Krishna, with the help of other influential members, would seek a meeting to be called according to the Constitution of the Party.

4. At the Central Committee meeting Nayak Dangoriya and Jeevan Krishna would vanquish the leader with their oratorical cunning.

5. During the meeting of the Central Committee, the members of the two factions would lay siege outside, and would keep shouting slogans, all demanding a change of leadership, in such a way that its noise would influence the proceedings inside.

6. At the meeting of the Central Committee, Jeevan Krishna would propose Nayak Dangoriya's name for the party leadership, and a sycophant would second that proposal. But it would be at this point that Jeevan Krishna's Krishna-like subtle and skilled wiliness would be used in a successful stranglehold or check. (Jeevan Krishna preferred the word 'check' to 'stranglehold'.) No proposal was fully acceptable without getting the extra-constitutional stamp of approval of the Korta, now living in exile. Doctor Haren was the interpreter and explainer of the Korta's sign language, and now that same Doctor

Haren was with Jeevan Krishna. This, therefore, was to be the import of the statement that Doctor Haren would gather from the Korta: he wished Jeevan Krishna, and not Nayak Dangoriya to take the place of the present Party Leader. Doctor Haren would arrive dramatically with the Korta's pronouncement at the very moment that Nayak Dangoriya's name was being proposed. Jeevan Krishna would meekly acquiesce to this order, and would display his sympathy towards Nayak Dangoriya in a respectful manner. There was also a deeper purport behind this stranglehold (or check). Without revolting against the extra-constitutional leadership of the Korta, this move would serve the important purpose of inactivating the Korta's control.

Jeevan Krishna respected the Korta's wisdom, but did not wish to be subjugated to his tacit leadership. From now on, Jeevan Krishna, with Doctor Haren's help, would himself present the import of all the Korta's statements. The sole aim of it all would be to strengthen the base of Jeevan Krishna's leadership.

Jeevan Krishna's mind was now as cheery as the ray of sunlight that entered through the gap in the curtains. Within a few hours, Doctor Haren would be returning with the import of the Korta's pronouncement for him. Every step of theirs was pre-planned. Under the combined demands of the supporters of both Jeevan Krishna and Nayak Dangoriya, the Party Leader had been forced to convene the meeting of the Central Committee. In the meantime, Jeevan Krishna had shown superb organizational skills in order to dislodge the Party Leader. He had just finished travelling from one end of the state to the other.

Indeed, he himself was surprised at his own oratorical prowess. It was almost as though his energy had doubled. The carbuncle on his thigh still troubled him a bit from time to time, but the ultimate goal of his conspiracy made him forget the pain. Just yesterday, he had very successfully spoken words of encouragement to the Party Leader at a meeting of the general members of the Party. After that, he had despatched Doctor Haren to get the Korta's blessings and sanction. The sanction that would arrive from the Korta was of course already known. Still, it was necessary to go and meet the Korta, or else there would be a lacuna in the stratagem.

As soon as he thought of Doctor Haren, it occurred to Jeevan Krishna that the doctor had said something to him before leaving. With its many meetings and discussions, the previous day had been such a busy one that Jeevan Krishna could not now recall what he had said. It had been something important. Even after trying for quite a while, the memory of the doctor's words eluded Jeevan Krishna. He felt uneasy.

Suddenly, a yawn came forth from his mouth. For quite some time now, he had been in the habit of yawning in this manner. Whenever some kind of disquieting or worrying thought entered his mind, he would yawn. Jeevan Krishna had had to face many uncomfortable situations, and many discomfiting thoughts in his public life. In his search for some kind of refuge from these thoughts, he had come to the yawn as a solution, and had begun to consciously practice it. That practice had become a habit now. In other words, Jeevan Krishna's yawns had long since ceased to have any connection with sleep, and were now connected, instead, with the state of unease in his mind.

After yawning, Jeevan Krishna felt the need to stretch, and straighten his legs. As soon as he unbent his knees, he felt a shooting pain from his carbuncle. Suddenly, he remembered what Doctor Haren had said to him the previous day. Aah! While listening raptly to the lusty ovations given to him by his followers, he had been so full of happiness that he had sat down abruptly on a ramshackle, broken-armed iron chair. A point from the damaged part of the chair had scratched his carbuncle, and made it bleed. Since Doctor Haren was nearby, he had immediately dressed it. But the doctor had had to start hurriedly on his trip to interview the Korta. Before leaving, he had told Jeevan Krishna to be sure to take an anti-tetanus injection, for the metal chair had been rusty. Without the shot, he would surely fall prey to tetanus. Doctor Haren had said that after interviewing the Korta, he would himself give Jeevan Krishna the necessary injection. The doctor had explained how agonizing tetanus or lockjaw was, and had mentioned that the first sign of it was when an open mouth could not be closed again. Even though Jeevan Krishna had heard the doctor say all this, he had not given it too much importance, since he had been extremely busy.

But at this point, Jeevan Krishna grew worried. What if the tetanus germs had entered his body by now? It would have been better if Doctor Haren had given him the injection before leaving yesterday.

Yawning, Jeevan Krishna stretched out the folds of his body. He tried to close his mouth. His heart missed a beat. Why was his mouth not closing? Had his nervous system lost control over his facial muscles? He tried once more. But his mouth remained agape. Frightened, Jeevan Krishna got up from his bed, and stood near the window. He did not try to close his mouth anymore, for he was convinced that by now, the tetanus germs had entered his body from the wound of his carbuncle, and had already begun their attack on his nervous system. Unless the doctor came and gave the antidote, the tetanus germs would spread all over his body. Jeevan Krishna would not have been too concerned about his bodily agony, but thinking of the political fallout of his illness made him panicky. Jeevan Krishna had the greatest faith in his own oratorical skills. But if his mouth remained ajar, he would lose that power of oratory. And today was the most important day in Jeevan Krishna's political life.

The time for the successful fruition of the subtle stratagem that he had plotted had arrived. He had unloosed an infallible arrow only after examining all the unwanted possibilities that could occur. But he had not calculated a medical crisis as being part of those possible obstacles.

Jeevan Krishna stretched out his hand to press the

bell beside the elegant bed, but paused. From now on, he would have to be very careful about how he conducted his work. As soon as he pressed the bell, it would be his domestic help who would come running, for at this time, his wife would definitely be busy in the puja room. He had no wish to acquaint his domestic help with his medical crisis. Especially now. If news of his ailment spread among his domestic workers, there was every possibility that his careful planning would become useless.

Jeevan Krishna tried to estimate just how much the malady had spread within his body. He did not feel any unnatural contractions from any other part of his body (he did not, however, have the courage to try and close his mouth again) so the disease had probably not attacked his entire body yet. Doctor Haren's presence was absolutely vital now. Like other important and powerful people within the party, Jeevan Krishna, too, thought of Doctor Haren as a very skilled physician. Doctor Haren had the antidote to this disease in his hands, and since just a portion of his body was afflicted with this malady, he would be able to cure it quite easily.

Consoling himself with his faith in the doctor, he began to attempt to think through the political fallout of this situation. Jeevan Krishna had written the script of the last ploy in the manner of the climax of a dramatic story, and that climax was to be played out at the Central Committee meeting, where, confronted by Jeevan Krishna's oratory, the Party Leader would be totally vanquished. Nayak Dangoriya's name would be proposed by him for the leadership, and breathlessly, at the very last moment, Doctor Haren would show up dramatically with the divine pronouncement of the Korta, and, to the accompaniment of the lusty cheers of all his supporters, Jeevan Krishna would be installed as the Party Leader.

But at this moment, Doctor Haren's presence was vital also for the treatment of his ailment. Even if he turned up on time, he would not come to Jeevan Krishna's house, for that was not how the events of the day had been planned!

So what could be done, then? Would the change in the last part of the drama spoil the attractiveness of its climax? But since there seemed to be no other way out, and since Jeevan Krishna himself controlled the whole drama, he would not lose his grip over the entire show if the scene of Doctor Haren's entry was changed somewhat. Instead of going straightaway to the meeting, Doctor Haren would first have to come to Jeevan Krishna's house, and they would go on to the meeting together. That moment, of their joint entrance, would now become the climax of the play, at the culmination of which the whole gathering would resound with the fresh demands of Jeevan Krishna's supporters. At that thrilling moment, Doctor Haren would communicate the purport of the Korta's divine pronouncement. Nayak Dangoriya's role would be rendered irrelevant, and Jeevan Krishna's supporters would, with their loud cheers, completely sideline Nayak Dangoriya, and, lifting Jeevan Krishna bodily, place him on the leader's chair.

Lost in pleased contemplation of the aesthetic beauty of this imagined scene, Jeevan Krishna with his mouth still agape, paused at the window for the first time, and tried to enjoy the natural beauty of the scene outside. Looking at the brilliant sunshine pouring down from the cloudless sky, he tried to banish the unhappiness that tried to crowd his mind, and waited for his wife's arrival. As far as the matter of plotting this stratagem went, she was not in his confidence, but she was needed now, for Doctor Haren would have to come from the railway station straight to his house, and it was his wife who would have to make the arrangements for that. Jeevan Krishna heard the weighty footsteps of his wife's portly frame outside the room. In the meantime, a bee entered through the open window, and began to hum around Jeevan Krishna's open mouth. While he was moving his head around so that the bee would not enter his gaping maw, the sound of his wife's voice came floating in, 'Here, are you listening? A person from the Party has come to meet you. He says he has something urgent to say. I've told him to come in here.'

Jeevan Krishna now became quite terrified. Wanting to tell his wife not to bring the man in here, he turned his face with its open mouth, now under attack from the bee, towards her, but realized that he could not speak with his mouth ajar like this. He therefore shook his head and hands violently, and ran to his wife's side. He tried to make her understand the gravity of the situation through desperate signs. But Jeevan Krishna had yet to fabricate a sign language for himself in the way that the Korta had done. As a result, his wife was bewildered and puzzled by the meaningless shaking of his hands and head.

In the meantime, a prefatory clearing of the throat was heard outside the door. Without delay, Jeevan Krishna banged the door shut, and turning, looked angrily at his wife. It was only then that his wife noticed Jeevan Krishna's yawning oral cavity, and realized that something untoward had happened. Her mouth, too, fell open with apprehension. Jeevan Krishna had always been irritated by the dimness of his wife's mental faculties. Today was no exception. But whereas, on other days, Jeevan Krishna would merely express his irritation on his face, and desist from anything else, today, upon encountering a hurdle in expressing that irritation, his anger increased even more. That anger manifested itself in a huge slap which he administered with his right hand, leaving a rosy imprint on his wife's rotund cheek. With that massive smack, her mouth shut of its own accord. A glimmer of intelligence appeared in her dull mind, and understanding the gravity of the situation, she whispered, 'The other Dangoriya has sent the man who's waiting outside. He wants to talk of some extremely urgent matter with you. What shall I do now? I'll bring you some paper and a pen, just write down what's wrong.'

The 'other Dangoriya', or the Other Respected Gentleman, that his wife had mentioned was the Party Leader. Jeevan Krishna momentarily forgot his bodily discomfort. His mind jumped with joy, for the meaning of sending a representative for talks could only mean that the Party Leader wished to come to an understanding. He must have had an attack of nerves at the prospect of his final defeat, and was making a last effort to bring his one-time trusted supporter within the ambit of his own sphere of influence. At this moment, Jeevan Krishna felt like insulting the Party Leader by ridiculing his representative with a refusal.

But his enjoyment was somewhat marred by the fact that the condition of his mouth did not afford him the opportunity to do so. However, the significance of sending the representative in this manner could only be that the Party Leader had formally acknowledged his moral defeat. Jeevan Krishna's mind filled with joy at the thought.

His wife proffered him pen and paper. Writing, Jeevan Krishna let her know that his mouth was ajar because tetanus germs had attacked his body. Doctor Haren was needed to treat him. But it was vital that no other doctor, or any other person, got even an inkling of this. His wife would personally have to speak on the telephone with Doctor Haren, so that he could finish his work speedily, and come to Jeevan Krishna's house. The representative of the Party Leader would have to be sent off without delay, with the excuse that Jeevan Krishna was at this moment busy at prayer, after which he would be going to the Central Committee meeting where he would meet the Party Leader.

It did not take long for Jeevan Krishna's wife to

establish a connection with Doctor Haren on the phone. The instructions that Doctor Haren gave after listening to the whole history, were

1. The patient should rest at this time.

2. He should not try unnecessarily to shut his open mouth.

3. Doctor Haren himself would make arrangements to cure the ailment on his return, and

4. There was no cause for worry.

Jeevan Krishna was bedridden. ('Bedridden': even though this description occurred to Jeevan Krishna, he felt the word to be tasteless). He realized that he would have to pass a few more hours in this kind of distress, but he did not get worried, for there was still ample time for the Central Committee meeting, and Doctor Haren would arrive much before it was due to start. Doctor Haren would cure him on his arrival here. The place of the Korta's exile was not all that far away. Doctor Haren could have gone in a motor-car, but the arrangement was to go to a place just a few stations away by train in order to safeguard the secrecy of the journey. The doctor would take about half an hour extra on his return train journey. But there was no cause for worry. With the arrival of Doctor Haren, the last scene of today's play would be inaugurated, and Jeevan Krishna's banner of victory would flutter proudly.

In his mind, Jeevan Krishna could already hear the renewed cheers and ovation of his supporters, and, disregarding his bodily discomfort, his mind was totally immersed in joy at the contemplation of his imagined success. Lying supine on his bed, Jeevan Krishna became engrossed in the imagined rehearsal of the final scene.

Suddenly, he heard Doctor Haren's voice at his ear. 'Aah, you had fallen asleep. Wake up, I've arrived. What's the matter with you?'

Jeevan Krishna woke up with a start, and hastily sat up on the bed. He realized that the thrills of joy that had flown through his body had been his dreams merely. His eyes went hastily to the clock. He saw that it was time for the Central Committee meeting to take place. He clutched Doctor Haren's hand, and signalled towards the door a couple of times. That is, they should start for the place where the meeting was to be held. But he remembered that his body harboured tetanus germs, and his mouth was ajar. The doctor should make arrangements to close his mouth. With the forefinger of his right hand, he pressed the lower lip of his open mouth, to indicate to the doctor and make him understand that…

But Jeevan Krishna started when his finger touched his mouth. It seemed his mouth had closed of its own accord! A thrill of joy went through his body. In a fever of happiness, Jeevan Krishna shouted, 'Doctor! Doctor! My illness has been cured!'

But before the words left his mouth, the doctor had already unloosed a question, 'Why, there's nothing whatsoever the matter with you, is there?' Both sentences crashed into each other midway. Both Jeevan Krishna and the doctor looked at each other for a moment, and paused. Jeevan Krishan saw a look of unconcern on the doctor's face, while on Jeevan Krishna's visage, the doctor saw a look of eager impatience, covered over with a patina of joy.

Jeevan Krishna said hurriedly, 'Doctor, there's no time to lose, the meeting has already started. Come, let's go there.'

The doctor was in no hurry. A laugh danced at the corners of his mouth, and vanished. But Jeevan Krishna did not even notice it. The doctor said, 'Aah, so you don't know? The meeting is over. The Party Leader changed both the venue and timing of the meeting, you see! It appears he had sent somebody over to let you know. But you did not see him. The Central Committee has reposed full faith in the Party Leader…'

What kind of explosive dialogue was this, emerging from Doctor Haren's mouth? What was this trembling in Jeevan Krishna's heart? Was this the same Doctor Haren, the man who was his accomplice?

Swallowing, Jeevan Krishna asked, 'But the Korta…'

The sentence remained unfinished, for he saw that the doctor was shaking his head from right to left. In other words, the articulation of the Korta's indicative language was simple, and its meaning terrible. Jeevan Krishna did not have the Korta's approval.

Once more, the doctor remarked, 'These people (meaning the Central Committee) have done something quite reprehensible, you know…it seems they have expelled you for six years…'

The sentence burst like a hundred hydrogen bombs in Jeevan Krishna's ears. A sympathetic sound issued forth from the doctor's lips, but a smile danced its way across the corners of his mouth. This time, the dance caught Jeevan Krishna's eye. It did not take long now for the full import of that dance to impress itself on Jeevan Krishna's mind.

The meaning of the situation was as clear as the bright light outside. Through Doctor Haren, Jeevan Krishna's stratagem had been defeated by the Korta's trickery. The drama, in whose imagined success Jeevan Krishna's mind had been so totally immersed, was perhaps Jeevan Krishna's script, but its direction had been in the Korta's hands all along. Jeevan Krishna had had no control over Doctor Haren's role. The Korta, the master of the party's fate, had already decided it beforehand.

In other words, Jeevan Krishna was the villain of the play that he himself had written! He could not make out where the climax of his own play was positioned. Did ever a stupid politician drown in this manner in his own boat in the canal of water that he himself had dug?

Suddenly, in the light of this knowledge, another suspicion assembled itself in Jeevan Krishna's mind. Had his mouth, which had been agape since the morning, been a tactic of Doctor Haren's, then?

Opening his mouth to ask Doctor Haren about this, Jeevan Krishna noticed that Doctor Haren had, in the meantime, exited from the stage.

Snake

The light of the sun plays hide and seek on the surface of the pond, full now to the brim. It is screened by trees. A partition made of split bamboo has been erected there. It is high noon. It is lonely here: there is nobody around.

Putoli keeps the bucket on the ground and, pausing near the screen, unhesitatingly takes off the clothes covering the upper part of her body. Along with her gamosa that she has been carrying in her hands, she keeps the bundle of clothes on the bamboo divider. She never takes off her petticoat. So what if there is a bamboo barrier? She has never been able to rid herself of this hesitation.

At this moment, her eyes fall on the chameleon. Perched on top of the stone washing slab, it is staring fixedly at her. Possibly, it has turned rosy because it has seen her naked body.

Dhet, why is she thinking in this manner? Putoli scolds the chameleon in her mind: Shoo, go away, you shameless creature. And indeed, it may even have heard her unspoken words for immediately, the chameleon leaps nimbly and vanishes from sight. Putoli is amused. The creature looks like an excited boy who has fled after being caught in some shameful act.

The bucket already contains water that she has fetched from the pond. She is about to lift the mug when her eye is drawn to something else. She gets the feeling that somebody is looking at her bare breasts. This time, it is not on the stone. A little distance from the edge of the pond are some toadstools. Nearby are clumps of fiddlehead ferns, growing wild. Behind the line of toadstools is a pair of eyes. A forked tongue hangs out greedily. As though it would lick her body if it could.

A pair of hungry eyes!

Is the snake looking at her? It is probably only waiting to pounce on a frog. It does not have a raised hood, so it is not a cobra. But she is extremely frightened of snakes. She looks fearfully at it for a while. It has not moved at all. In any case, the snake is still some distance away. If necessary, she can rush to safety by the side of the bamboo barrier. Quickly, she begins to pour water over herself. On other days, she takes a long time over her bath, scrubbing herself thoroughly. Sometimes, she washes her hair with the seeds of monisal. She scrubs off the grime on her feet and armpits with a loofah made from a sponge gourd.

She likes to idle a bit during her bath. It is only at this time that she touches her own body. It is a flawless body, fair, glowing, slender. God has been generous in giving her this body. She devotes this time in the afternoons to herself. She lavishes a great deal of care on her body as she scrubs it till it glows.

But for whom is she lavishing all this care? Who knows what has happened to her young husband these days. All he knows is work, work, and more work. Does that body with its powerful chest harbour any love for her? The blood in his veins seems to have become chill and cold.

The snake seems to be satisfied. Opening her eyes again after washing off the soap from her face, Putoli notices that the snake has gone away from behind the toadstools. After wiping herself dry with the gamosa, she comes out from behind the bamboo screen. Just as she is about to enter the house by the back veranda, she sees the snake once more. This time, however, the snake is not rooted to the spot, staring at her. Its hungry tongue is still flicking this way and that. But what is this? Looping its body along the side of the wall, the snake is moving towards the house. She watches the snake go into the house through a rat hole in the ground.

Unknown to herself, a scream escapes her: 'Aaah!'

A few boulders have been put down on the main road. That must mean that the panchayat or other such local body has become active here. Quite a lot of improvements have taken place here within this last one year. The whole place seems somehow more spacious. Even though the houses are scattered around with large spaces between them, this area is now an outlying part of the village itself.

Kameswar is pleased. He enjoys the company of other people. No thought of settling down ever enters his mind. Like a grasshopper, he leaps about from one house to another. If his long nose gets even a whiff of the scent of domesticity, he flees. The heady scent of tobacco, the warm, flavourful aroma of lentils tempered with spices, the fragrance of a courtyard washed down with cowdung and water, the milky smell of the cowshed—whenever he gets even a hint of these domestic scents, he gets a warm feeling of intimacy. Admittedly, the scent of a woman, so like that of freshly-garnered grain, enters his nostrils and knocks against some part of his heart, arousing a different kind of feeling in him. But he is not the type to settle into domesticity. Instead, he is a free-flying kite. But he does not mind sticking around if somebody else's woman pours on him the nectar of her honeyed looks. When that nectar dries up and evaporates, he, too, vanishes.

After having dined on prison fare for a year, Kameswar is now back. The coral tree in the courtyard catches his eyes from quite a distance. Well, well, the house now sports a tin roof. The pillars, too—are they wooden ones? So much progress, in just a year! Twelve months ago, he had had a slight feeling of affection towards Lokkhi, the daughter of Sodanath, a refugee. For a free-flying kite, it had been but a brief pause.

The coral tree in Lokkhi's courtyard is now in full

bloom. He had lost his head on just such a day, when the coral tree had been in full flower. No, it had not been over Lokkhi. She had responded to his love. But who knows what had got into him one day? He had felt the irresistible urge to explore others' pockets in a railway platform that was quite empty of crowds. Is there anything that he had not turned his hand to? A broker for a goat-seller, a cowherd in a cowshed, a pedlar selling brassware...He had even, in fact, worked for a while with the Marwari businessman Jhamanlal. He had tried all these trades. But suddenly, that day, he had felt the irresistible urge to learn this art, as well. He had barely put his hand into the pocket before he was nabbed. And then, a stay as a guest of the government in prison. Admittedly, he had stayed there in some comfort. Kameswar had the gift of storytelling, of embroidering facts. The amazing stories that he wove seemed absolutely real. People listened to him, spellbound. He had even spread out the wares of his riveting tales before the jailor. That worthy had fallen a bit under the spell of Kameswar's tales.

He had charmed Lokkhi, too, with his stories. Painting all the astonishing happenings of the world in such vivid colours, he had told his stories in such a way that they had glittered with an irresistible lustre. Now, he was returning after a year in prison. Before even considering where he should go, he had remembered Lokkhi. It is two hours by the slow, rattling train. But it is three hours again from the station. So what? He has been hearing the music of Lokkhi's body this last one year. This is the reason for his return. On seeing the red flowers of the coral tree, he begins to sing the famed Bhupen Hazarika song, 'They say that the blossom of the coral tree…' With a sense of buoyant cheeriness, he begins to hum the song, and moves towards the house.

He hears the scream at that moment. As soon as he reaches the gate, he hears someone crying out, 'Aaah!'

It is lonely here. The house is closed from outside. Is that Lokkhi's scream? He has forgotten the sound of her voice. It is, nevertheless, the sound of a woman's terrified scream. Who knows what calamity has befallen somebody? He rushes into the courtyard of the house.

Putoli is taken aback on seeing a stranger suddenly materialize in front of her in this way. She is returning from the pond after her bath, and her clothes are still in disarray. She has remained rooted to the spot after seeing the snake enter her house. And now here is this strange man, appearing out of nowhere in front of her. He seems to have entered her compound after hearing her scream. She is very embarrassed.

Kameswar, too, realizes that the woman in front of him is another man's wife. She is not Lokkhi at all. But what beauty! The experienced Kameswar, who has sipped the nectar of many different flowers, has seen many a stunning beauty. But this woman in front of him is like a flame. His gaze rests briefly on her face. Her complexion resembles the rosy hue of milk mixed with sindoor. His restless gaze slips down to the curve of her breasts. Slithering further down, his look fastens itself on her navel. Beneath her damp clothes, that part of her body is creamy white.

Putoli's heart is thumping loudly in her breast, as though it is a threshing-pedal. A snake has entered her house. Her eyes are glazed with fear. She has no time to observe where the stranger's gaze has fallen. She merely gestures towards her house, and swallowing hard, says, 'Snake.'

From her manner, Kameswar realizes that a snake has entered her house. At that moment, his mind is filled with the distillation of many nectars. Even while his eyes explore her body, he begins to move towards the back door. He will kill the snake.

Suddenly, Putoli comes to her senses. A stranger is about to enter her house! She says hastily, 'No, no, there's no need...the snake must have gone away by now.' But her heart is still thumping with fear.

What will Kameswar do now? His feet are gummed to the ground, as though with sticky jackfruit paste. His mind, too, is full of inquisitiveness. If this is not Lokkhi, who is she? And where have Lokkhi and her family vanished? He also realizes that he is thirsty. His throat is parched with thirst. He asks her, 'Will you give me a drink of water?' He uses the familiar tumi to address her, rather than the honorific apuni. Here is a strange, married woman in front of him, a woman who belongs to another. But Kameswar, who thinks of the world as his oyster and who is quite at home anywhere he finds himself, has never addressed anybody of the opposite gender with the respectful apuni.

She hurriedly bids him to sit in the veranda outside the house. A murha is already placed there. He sits on the low cane stool. Even though her fear of the snake has not yet gone, Putoli screws up her courage and enters the house to fetch water. While she is away, Kameswar sits on the murha and ponders on how to stretch this encounter a bit. His memory of Lokkhi is now becoming hazy. A different picture is forming deliciously in front of his eyes.

Does it take so long to have a drink of water? Putoli reflects that the man is sipping on the water as slowly as though he is drinking tea. While handing him the glass, the anchal had slipped from her breast. Since then, Kameswar's face and eyes have been aflame. Can this fire be doused by a mere glassful of water? He asks for one more glass. While sipping the water, he unknots his bundle of stories.

In the course of his conversation, he finds out about Lokkhi and her people. Lokkhi's father, the refugee Sadanath, has sold the land and relocated to a new place near the hills. Many refugees have cleared land there and settled in those places. Putoli tells him that it's been a year since they've come here. Her husband has bought this land, with the house. The tin roof has been added by her husband himself.

Putoli remains standing, but her graceful body with the slender waist dances in Kameswar's mind's eye. He spins out the time by opening the bundle of stories. His thirst for water has been slaked, now what other kind of thirst can he express? He asks for an areca nut and a paan leaf. 'Can I have a tamol, do you think?'

Whether it was from the juice of the areca nut that she brought him, or whether it was from the touch of her fingers, his body begins to quiver. Deep in conversation, Kameswar's lips redden and spittle slips down from the sides of his chin. He tells her the story of how this spot was once a dense Reserved Forest, how fearless hunters would hunt down tigers with muzzle loading guns. (Tiger hunting with muzzle loading guns! In Kameswar's tales, bullets come out of muzzle loading guns!) He, too, was once in the camps with the hunters. Of course he omits to mention that he was with the smugglers who shot game illegally here merely in the capacity of a porter who would ferry their guns. His tales hint, instead, that he himself had personally despatched leopards and other big cats.

Has he brought with him the orbs of those big cats in his own eyeballs? The fire from those orbs licks at the contours of Putoli's body. Putoli has observed this. But his stories are irresistible, riveting. She is unaware of the passing of time as he sits there, spinning his tales in front of her. Only when her stomach begins to rumble with hunger does she realize that the sun has gone to the west of the coral tree. She becomes edgy.

At last, Kameswar gets up. He packs up his bundle of stories. Coming down from the veranda to the courtyard, he pauses for a while, and says, 'The snake may still be inside the house. Take care. I know the ojha, a powerful shaman who can charm a snake and bring it out from your house. I'll bring him along tomorrow. Who can say about snakes? As the saying goes, tigers attack on sight; snakes, when fated, bite.'

Kameswar leaves. A few blossoms fall from the coral tree to the ground. But the way in which Kameswar has put the fear of the serpent in Putoli's mind paralyzes her. She is quite unable to go inside the house now. She remains on the veranda, awaiting her husband's arrival.

Moniram is a vigorous man with a fit, muscular body. For the last three years, it has been as though everything he has touched with his industrious hands has turned to gold. A year ago, he shifted to this place. A lot of land had become available after the jungle was cleared. He, too, has established some fields here. Handing over his old plot to his brothers, he came here with the intention of overseeing his fields from close quarters.

It seems that Lakshmi, the goddess of prosperity knows the way into his home. The fields have yielded bumper harvests for the last three years. His mind seems to have become wild with this abundance of prosperity. This year, in a fit of reckless courage, he has taken a timber stand. Already, he is seeing it fetch him amazing returns. He is now dreaming of becoming a Mahajan—a timber merchant and contractor. He has heard that a timber mill is on sale. The owner of the mill, Jhamanlal, is going away from here. Moniram had gone to see him. However, he was unable to meet Jhamanlal, for the mill is now closed.

He has heard that Jhamanlal has set up his establishment in the town. He is determined to have the mill. After seeing it, his mind is aflame with desire. He cannot wait to get his hands on it.

It is quite late by the time he returns. The sun is already setting when he reaches the entrance to his home. From the path itself he sees Putoli sitting in the veranda. Poor thing, she is looking out for his return.

Only on reaching the veranda does he realize the actual reason why she has gone without her meal. (He has already told her to have her meal without him if he is late. He leaves for work early in the morning, after having a hearty meal.) As soon as he steps on the veranda, Putoli leaps up and hugs him close. From her fearful, breathless account of what had happened, Moniram understands that a snake has entered the house. What a simpleton this girl is! How can the snake remain inside this long? It must have come inside to catch a rat and gone out by now. Still, to reassure her, he lifts the bamboo bar that keeps the door shut, and enters the house. He finds no trace of the snake even after a thorough search of the house.

The fear has not yet left Putoli's mind. Who knows in which corner of the house it is lurking? However, taking courage from Moniram's presence, she enters the house. By the time they finish their meal, it is late.

Putoli's imagination sprouts wings when her tired body lies on the bed. Curled up against Moniram's chest, she tries to warm herself. The gentle aroma of his body arouses her. Tonight, fearing the snake, she has kept the lantern lit with a dim light. A ray of light falls faintly on his face. She wants him to clasp her in his warm arms and draw her into the honeycomb in his heart. She is, after all, his honey.

The dim light of the lantern plays hide and seek with the shadows. His face, too, does the same. Putoli cannot read the expression on it. In his wide-awake eyes is the tantalizing vision of the soil of the fields he wants to acquire. His mind searches for clods of gold in the field. He seems to have forgotten all about the honeypot nestling near him.

A volcano lies dormant in Putoli's veins. She snuggles closer to him. His muscular body fills her own with a fiery heat. With delicate fingers, she begins to trace the down that marks a path from his chest in a line. The fear of the snake had kept her from entering her house. But now she desires Moniram's muscular body to twine round her own, like a snake. Once before, too, she had seen a pair of poisonous gom snakes coiled around each other. Oblivious to all else, the two of them had lain, coiled and entwined around each other. She had shuddered at the sight, even then. As she remembers the scene now, she feels no fear. She wants to become Moniram's serpent-seductress. The blood in her veins is fevered. Perhaps Moniram has heard the call of her body. Suddenly, he hugs her very strongly.

Moniram seems to be a clockwork toy. As soon as the clockwork mechanism winds down, the toy stands immobile. His body becomes still again within two quick minutes, as though this is some kind of a thirst for water. Gulp down a glass of water hastily, and quench one's thirst. Abandoning her body, he turns over on his side and, snoring lustily, goes off to sleep.

Putoli, however, cannot sleep. The blood in her veins, her body itself, is fevered. Moniram has not even recognized the words of her body's language. This seems to have become the norm these days. The touch of his hands has become dulled. With an unsatisfied sigh, Putoli, too, turns over to the other side to sleep.

Moniram awakes even before the birds do. He is an extremely busy man. The luxury of sleep, however, does not leave Putoli so soon. In any case, she falls asleep quite late. But Moniram is after all her beloved. It makes her happy if she can send him out for his day's work with a good meal in his belly. It appears that today, he will go in search of Jhamanlal's new place of work straightaway. He keeps talking about the mill. For some time now, he has been quite obsessed with the mill. He will be quite late in returning today, as well.

Putoli had told him about the stranger and that he is supposed to bring a shaman with him today. It will be better if Moniram is at home when they arrive. She feels that the snake is still around inside the house somewhere. If he leaves, how can she remain indoors? He laughs, and says, 'There's no danger, you foolish girl, don't you know that snakes don't hang around inside houses?'

The soaring kite that is Kameswar's mind has now found a new place to rest. He had come here looking for a refugee girl called Lokkhi. Another picture has been superimposed on that image now. He has brought along with him a famed shaman. He reaches the coral tree. The sun has paused at the threshold of the sky, and is watching with open eyes. Has Mister Sun glimpsed the inside of Kameswar's flaming eyes?

Putoli sees the stranger while he is still a good way off. With him is another man, probably the shaman. From the courtyard itself Kameswar shouts, 'I'm thirsty. Fetch me a glass of water!' Talking nineteen to the dozen, he tries to enter the house. Putoli hurriedly places a murha on the veranda and bids him sit down there. While bringing him the glass of water, Putoli adjusts her clothes so that her body is well covered. The way the man ogles at her…! It's as though all her clothes will not shield her from his hungry eyes.

After gulping down the water, Kameswar asks her, 'Isn't your husband at home, then? If he had been in, he would have seen the expertise of the famous ojha. Just watch, all the snakes in this house will be caught now.'

She wants to ask him, 'How come you look at me in the same way as that snake does? Will the ojha be able to capture that look, as well?'

The learned ojha is now busy going about his preparations for capturing the snake. In his hands, there is nothing else besides a stick. Will he capture the snake with that, then? Kameswar's bundle of tales has, in the meantime, been opened. Has the juice from the betel-nut she has given him flushed his face and reddened his eyes? The man can really tell a tale. His gaze is fixed unwaveringly on her. Indeed, she finds herself unable to move away, as she listens, mesmerised, to his colourful stories.

The learned ojha really has captured a snake. He has found it in the area on the other side of the pond. Holding down its head with his stick, he picks up the snake with his bare hands, and puts it into a bag. As she watches the bag shake from the snake's agitated movements, she feels her body quiver. The ojha says, 'It's a highly poisonous snake. Nothing less than a spectacled cobra…'

Cobra! That means the snake that has entered her house is not this one. Is that snake still inside, then? Her scream of fright remains confined to the limits of her mind. She does not wish to display her fear to these strangers now. The success in capturing the snake brings a smile to Kameswar's face. The triumph evident there is almost as though he has conquered an entire kingdom. After gulping down tea from her brass baanbati, he goes away with the learned ojha and the snake. 'I'll have to keep coming this way, you know. I'll drop in sometimes. I'd like to meet your husband, as well…'

Kameswar is not the type to wait around for the husband to come back, in expectations of meeting him. After being released from prison, he is now, once more, engaged in working for a contractor who supplies mutton to a military camp situated some miles away. Kameswar's job is to search out goats. With the excuse of hunting around for suitable goats, he goes to the fields and gets acquainted with Moniram.

Kameswar's skinny appearance contrasts oddly with Moniram's vigorous good looks and his rippling muscles. Moniram, who is blessed with a golden touch, now has dreams of becoming a rich merchant. Kameswar perceives this fact after talking with Moniram, who is set on buying Jhamanlal's closed mill.

Jhamanlal's mill. Why, some time ago, Kameswar was Jhamanlal's manager! (In reality, he was only a lowly labourer.) Of course, he could definitely introduce Moniram to Jhamanlal. Now where is Jhamanlal's new place of business? Kameswar will find out, for Moniram's sake, he will find out.

The coral tree has shed its leaves. It is bare of blossoms, as well. New leaves have grown in again. The year has come full cycle. And now, blossoms are budding on the shrub once more. Kameswar, a resting bee, has spent this last year here. He is still hunting around for Jhamanlal's gaadi. As soon as he finds it, he will take Moniram there. He is a daily visitor to Moniram's house. Putoli hates the way he stares at her. He asks for a drink of water as soon as he arrives. The man has such a thirst! He always tries to enter the house. Putoli, however, always places the cane murha on the veranda for him. Things have been going on in this way.

One day, Putoli sees a cast-off snakeskin outside the kitchen. She feels extremely fearful. When she tells

Moniram about it, he laughs uproariously. He says, 'You idiot, that's not a new skin. Some bird has flown in with it, and dropped it here. One has to live with snakes in places like these. It won't do to be so scared, you know!'

Moniram is in high spirits. His mind is chugging along cheerfully like a new locomotive. It seems Jhamanlal will sell the mill. Kameswar has brought him this news. It has taken Kameswar a long time to search out Jhamanlal's new place of business. Well, never mind the time taken, at least it's good news.

After having an early meal on Sunday, Moniram tells Putoli, 'Get ready. We'll go to the Sunday haat.' The weekly market is about five miles away. While going there, Moniram will show her the mill. And he will buy her a new pair of clothes at the haat.

The mill is not visible from where the passengers alight. It comes into view only after they walk on for a while. What is there to see? It is just a timber mill, after all. The dusty machines are festooned with dirty cobwebs. Everything is in a shambles. Putoli can see nothing appealing about the mill at all.

Standing outside the mill, suddenly, her gaze falls on Moniram's face. She is startled. What kind of expression is that in his eyes? He is staring fixedly at the mill. Who is that nymph who, with charmed arrows has lighted that fire in his eyes? Is that mill more addictive, then? Does it hold a greater allure than this body of hers? The memory of the restlessness of her agitated body at night comes to Putoli's mind. This lustful expression in the eyes of the man who has not even given a glance to her own flawless, milk-white body! She gets restless and fidgety. Moniram's infatuated eyes remain fixed unwaveringly on the mill. In her breast is the fever of another kind of fire. It is as though the flames of that fire will leap out and reduce the mill itself to ashes.

Storyteller Kameswar's tales are gradually becoming shorter. Even the amazing, astonishing stories are becoming brief. In reality, it had not taken Kameswar very long to find Jhamanlal's new place of business. He had tarried only because he had seen a new honeycomb. He, however, could not gain access to the inner chamber of the comb's queen bee. He has now given up hope. It is now time for him to take wing. Let Jhamanlal's mill become Moniram's. When he comes near the coral tree, he muses that he will leave today, just after drinking his glass of water. From beyond the gate, he calls out as he always does, 'Are you at home, then?'

Putoli has seen him from afar. That fellow! He's come again. He always comes when Moniram is not around. Maybe today, she'll tell him not to come when Moniram is not at home. Out of sheer habit, he stands on the veranda and says, 'Well, then, give me a glass of water.' Today, he walks towards the murha on the veranda on his own. He does not stare at her eyes, as he does on other days.

The picture of Moniram as he stands in front of the mill is still in Putoli's mind. She goes into the house absently to fetch the water, but pauses at the door. What's happening to her…she is afraid of the snake within. The snake of her imagination is shedding its skin there, getting a new one. Pausing at the door, Putoli looks straight at Kameswar, and says, 'Come on, come inside.'

With his lips on the tumbler of water, Kameswar's eyes fall on the coral tree. Today, it is bright with scarlet flowers! Far away, on a loudspeaker there is the sound of a song. It is a verse of a Bihu song, 'Dehore bhitorot asey…' There is, within the body…

The record has got jammed.

Romantic

There's been a request to write a story. My mind is usually so slothful that even though I keep thinking that I will write, no story gets penned. But when there's a request for a story, there's pressure on me, and I quickly dash one off. Most of my stories have been written in this manner. (The word that I have used to denote the request that's made on these occasions, 'formaish', is not an Asomiya one. Most likely the spelling is wrong. But this kind of word pops up in the stream of my stories, and I make use of it. Some of my writer friends tell me that fiction writers, or poets, can take this kind of liberty and use words in this manner. Good. And another thing. While writing a story, when subject, object, verb all become arranged in a sentence, I think I as the writer am in control of those words. But the funny thing is that when the controller of words begins to take liberties with the language and makes his own rules, he loses control over them. I don't mind this, either. When I write obscenities, and others abuse me, I say that it is not I who have written those words. It is the story that has demanded their use. When I write about wicked people, I can recognize similarly wicked people in my real life. If there is a similarity between what I have written and your real life, then that similarity is simply a coincidence. Does anybody else, besides a story writer, have this kind of wonderful freedom to abrogate all responsibility?)

But today, while settling down in the open veranda of my house to write a story, I keep remembering you. Repeatedly. Don't be afraid. I'm not about to make you the heroine of my story.

There's a creeper that climbs up the pillar of my veranda. I don't know its name. Bunches of red flowers cover the creeper in winter. Now, in the rainy season, deep green leaves have appeared, strong and fresh. But for some days now, I have been noticing a rather wonderful sight.

An adorable little bird is building her nest there. Well, not building it, but adorning it. The nest has actually been there for a long time. A family of small red munias had nested there last year. They have flown off somewhere, and are not around now. Since the last few days though, this sweet little bird has started to come to this nest. In this rainy season, the lawn in front of my veranda is filled with tall weeds. Since the rain has made the soil soggy and soft, I have not been able to weed the lawn for quite some time now. This new bird is adorning her nest, weed by single weed, which she brings in her beak.

Just look now, how I have feminized the bird, by adding the feminine suffix 'joni' to the word 'sorai,' 'bird'.

After all, I can't make out by looking at her, whether this bird is a man or a woman. You must be amused at the phrase 'man or woman.' But if birds could speak like people, they, too, would probably have used respectful words like these to denote masculinity or femininity. Somehow, the words 'male' and 'female' do not seem to be respectful. However, nobody has actually decreed that these words should have meanings different from the words 'man' and 'woman'. The shades of difference that these two words denote have been bestowed on them by our feelings, moulded by the culture that we live in.

Ah, I seem to have wandered away quite a bit from the main topic. As I was saying then—why is it that I have assumed the little bird to be a woman? But then mine, after all, is a man's mind. The bird is 'adorning' her nest. That bit of work we have kept inviolate for women. If this bird, instead of adorning her nest, had constructed or built it, then perhaps the little bird would have been a man in my eyes. But listen, this little bird really does belong to the tribe of women. While I was sitting on the veranda today and thinking of my story, I noticed another bird fluttering around, trying to capture her attention. He fluttered near her, moving to and fro with strange postures. However, she did not pay any attention to him. She remained busy, engrossed in carrying the weeds, one by one, to beautify her nest.

Now why have I assumed the other bird to be a man? Well, isn't his behaviour like a young man's? They follow young girls to catch their attention in the same manner.

It seems as though behaviour matches gender, always. Yes, well now, I've taken the word gender from grammar, okay?

After a while, I noticed the man bird lose heart in his efforts to get the woman bird to pay attention to him. He moved a little away from her, and began to search for something to eat on the lawn. The woman bird remained engrossed in her work. But the man bird's mind was still full of desire. Under the pretext of foraging among the weeds, he tried to hop closer to her. But the woman bird cold shouldered him. Oh, just look, how the term 'cold shoulder' has crept into this story. Does it look odd beside the other words, all dressed in sober clothes? But what can I do? Since the word has slipped in, let it remain, right?

Let me go back to the two little birds. The man bird continued his efforts. The woman bird suddenly flew into the nest. The man bird went and perched sadly on the branch of a nearby tree. Do you know the thought that came to my mind then? Why is this bird beautifying her nest? Does she not need a family? Or at least a companion? What kind of life will she have all alone in that beautifully decorated nest? In that case, why is she rejecting this bird that is so passionately in love with her? After all, he has done all he can to show her his love.

While I was thinking along these lines, one more thought came to my mind. Perhaps the little bird did not like the man bird's exhibitionist nature. But then, the very nature of man is such. Still, I realized that the woman's heart inside the bird viewed the man's nature with suspicion. While pondering on this matter, suddenly, I remembered you.

Both of us were mature people when we met. I do not know how the feeling of love in my heart was sparked. Still, at that age, my mind ought not to have become as restless as a youth's. Perhaps, without my being aware of it, that restlessness was expressed in my behaviour. I do not know if I got any hints from you to approach. But the kinds of excuses I would cook up to be in your vicinity, the kinds of ploys I would take recourse to! But somehow, I had assumed that since I was expressing my feelings of love, I would surely get a response from you. After all, mine is a man's mind! When a man wants something from a woman, it is routinely assumed that she is bound to give it. Since I was attracted to you, I had assumed that you would not remain unresponsive. It is not that I am of immature mind. Others have noticed that in all other matters I am a calm, thoughtful person. But the love that entered my heart brought with it the rush of youth to my veins.

But worse, one day I behaved like a callow youth. Meaning to attract you to me, one day, with a naive teenager's eagerness, I went and asked you a question. I do not remember the words, or the kinds of sentences I used, but the gist of my question was: what is your reply to all the different kinds of messages from the heart that I have been sending you?

Perhaps no mature person would have acted in this

manner. Perhaps people bound by the behavioural codes dictated by norms of conduct do not question things in this manner. The answers to these questions often come in the form of delightful experiences. This was the reason why my question had the lad's eagerness, in the same way that the first experiences and first occurrences in a young man's life make him pester his guardians for the reasons behind them.

Your reply had not been to my liking. You had said something like, 'It's best if that secret remains with me…'

I had tried to understand these words, imbuing them with all kinds of meanings. My eagerness increased the way one gets thirsty after eating something that has an astringent taste. The possible explanations of your reply took me along diverse paths. I had wondered if you had given me that mysterious, astringent reply in order to increase the thirst of my feelings for you.

Today, as I observe the drama of the birds before me, the motivation of our relationship comes differently to my mind. The woman bird has not been able to easily accept the exhibitionist behaviour of the man bird. She suspects the genuineness of his feelings. I realize now that perhaps you could not take my eagerness in your stride. You suspected this male behaviour. Perhaps this is a woman's normal response. The behaviour of the woman bird is giving me some clear signals.

However, I am remembering a story. Just now I told you that my final behaviour was immature, like a youth's. While saying this, I remembered the story of a youth, the story of a particular experience. The incident is true. But when it is enclosed within the bounds of sentences, with specific subjects, predicates and verbs, it becomes a story. This is why I am calling it a story.

The young man's days were of unalloyed happiness. He looked around at the world before him with enthusiasm, and he saw waves of joy everywhere. The pace of life around him was slow. He lived in a decent house in a growing town. His house shared a wall with another, the two houses having once been built as one unit. But later, a long brick wall had been erected to partition the large house into two smaller units. These were then sold to two different people. The young boy's family lived in one of these. The owner of the other house had let it out. This other house had remained vacant for a long time. Even though it was a developing town, there was no arrangement for piped water there. Each home therefore had to make its own arrangements for a regular supply of water, through wells or tube wells. There was a well behind the young boy's house. Nearby was a sacred pipal tree, to which flocked a variety of birds. This portion of the backyard was secluded. The boy loved the spot, which was separated from the other house by a wall of brick and cement. Perhaps, during construction, mortar had not been properly applied to the wall. A crack had developed in it.

Since the other house was vacant, it was always silent in this part. The young boy would spend the afternoon hours beside this well, looking at the antics of the birds on the pipal tree, and grimacing and making faces at his own reflection in the water of the well. This solitary time was his private space. Later, when he would grow up to be a poet, this daily span of private time would perhaps serve to inspire him.

One day, while he was solitarily communing with his own reflection in the well, a snatch of melody floated to his ear. It was being hummed by a human voice. Surprised, he looked around, and realized that the humming was coming from the other side of the wall. So somebody had come to that house which had been vacant for so long. He went forward curiously, and looked through the crack in the wall. An unusual sight rooted his feet to the ground. A look of amazement descended on his eyes, his face grew flushed. He saw that a temporary bath house had been constructed with bamboo matting on the other side.

A young woman, several years older than him, was humming and having a bath. The solitariness of the afternoon hour, combined with the privacy afforded by the bamboo matting had made her shed any hesitations or reservations that she may have had. The young woman had uncovered her entire body while bathing.

The boy had seen many beautiful scenes before, and had been enthralled by them. When he had gone to Guwahati, he had witnessed the beautiful sunset over the Brahmaputra. He had seen the splendid beauty of lightning lancing through a monsoon sky. His father had once shown him the sight of the mountain peaks of

Arunachal exposed to the elements and the sky above. But today, the unique attraction of a woman's body bewildered his mind and body. The joy of witnessing this beauty filled his heart with a strange, sweet pain that made his mind and body tremble.

Much later, when this young boy would see Botticelli's 'Venus' for the first time, he would remember the sweetly painful beauty of that body. In his mature years, a sense of proportion would come to him, and he would think of the creator of a woman's beauty as an even greater artist than Botticelli.

He was unaware of how long he gazed, stunned, at the beautiful sight before him. When he came to his senses, he felt an acute sense of guilt at having thus secretly looked at the nakedness of the woman. His limbs began to tremble. The conflict in his mind between the joy of witnessing such beauty, and the chastisement of guilt numbed him for the rest of the day.

The teenager had not committed this act intentionally. When, out of curiosity, he had peered through the crack in the wall, he had never thought that a sight such as this would meet his eyes. Perhaps, in due course, Time would have wiped out all traces of this act from his mind. He would have seen the beauty of a woman's naked body in the normal course of events, when he was older. He would not have suffered from any feeling of guilt then. He would liken a woman's ripe body to the beauty of a river in full flow, and declare the former to be the winner.

In comparison, the memory of that first glimpse of a woman's body would become dim.

But an incident occurred which heightened the teen's guilt further. Next day, at a social occasion in his own home, he was forced to come face to face with the young girl. The newly arrived neighbours next door had come to meet his family. The girl was an ideal of polite and correct behaviour. Her dress was careful, her behaviour courteous, and there was a natural sobriety in her gait and posture. There was good taste in her manners. Her guardians had tried to raise her as an ideal representative of civilized social norms.

Very soon, the two families became close. The girl did not have a younger brother, and in the natural course of things, she began to look on the youth as her younger sibling. She began to rely on him in the same way as she would have on her own brother. In those days, girls were diffident about going alone to visit others, or to the market. Society was still rather backward in this regard. When she had to go somewhere, therefore, the girl depended on the teenager to escort her. In this way, she became the young boy's Baideo, elder sister.

Off and on, however, the memory of that first glimpse would enter his disobedient mind unbidden, like an uninvited guest. That scene he had witnessed was inconsistent with the purity of their easy relationship. For this reason, his feelings of guilt were acute. One day, when these feelings became very strong, he decided that he would confess to what he had unknowingly done, and ask for her forgiveness. After this, he would wipe off all traces of that scene that kept entering the mirror of his mind.

Accordingly, one day he really did go up to her, and confessed to what he had done. He had assumed that she would accept this frank confession without any fuss, and the cordial bond between them would remain as strong as before, and his Baideo's trust in him would only increase. But, to his astonishment, his Baideo's reaction had been just the opposite.

Even while listening to him, she had flushed deeply. Abruptly, she had given him a sound slap on his face, and left. The youth had been astounded. He had not understood the reason for this reaction of hers.

Next day, her behaviour had once more become quite natural and easy. She spoke to him in the same way as before, and asked him to accompany her someplace. In his mind's eye, the youth suddenly saw a firmament darkening with clouds, and then, just as suddenly, clearing up again.

But the young boy would grow up one day. He would find new explanations to replace many old ones. Another explanation for his Baideo's behaviour would enter his mind. The reason for her sudden eruption of anger was not that a man—even though he was a teenager—had looked upon her body. By doing so, he had wronged her, for he had no right to do so. If, at that time, she had seen that thirsty gaze drinking in her beauty, she would perhaps not have said anything, but hastened away from the place. But when the youth confessed to what he had done, his words had exposed her in a different manner. Growing up as she had, she had veiled the natural woman within herself with the cover of socially accepted manners. The boy's words had ripped that veil off. The carefully nurtured refinement that had created this woman had become confused on coming face to face with this secret woman within her—the one that wished to be thrilled by the male gaze on the luxuriant beauty of her body.

Her slap had not been aimed at the youth's cheek. It had been aimed at those words which had pierced through her privacy, and had revealed the naked woman within her body. The young boy would find consolation in this explanation, but would not know whether it was true or not.

While I was telling you the story of this young boy, the memory of the explanation of a sentence you had spoken to me came to my mind. I was telling you the antics of a pair of birds before I recounted the story of the young boy.

Now I am also beginning to get another explanation. I think that the screen of correct behaviour around your natural self veils your mind. I had tried to rip apart that veil with the lance of male behaviour, and searched for the natural woman within. My incoherent behaviour and question had aimed to smash and shatter the screen of correctness over your mind. You had become alert, and readjusted that screen carefully over your psyche. Is this explanation of your words, 'It's best if that secret remains with me…' not correct, then? Oh, I forgot, you won't tell me. Of course, the one who spoke the sentence will not give the explanation. But if the person who accepts it receives it in his own way, the one who spoke cannot control it.

I was supposed to have been writing a story. Instead, here I am, writing stuff to you. Perhaps you wish to say, what is all this nonsense? (Abol tabol, nonsense. Is abol tabol an Asomiya word, I wonder? Well, what's the harm in using a borrowed word that conveys the appropriate meaning?)

Wait, wait a minute. While telling you all this, I quite forgot to look at the drama of the birds, and find out what's happening there. Now I am looking at the birds again. The show involving them continues, but in a somewhat modified form. The woman bird is as busy as before in bringing in bits of greenery in her beak to adorn the nest. She is engrossed in this task. The man bird has changed his strategy. He is not dancing around her in the same agitated way as before to show her his emotions. Instead, he is hopping towards the nest a step at a time, slowly and cautiously. The woman bird flutters into the nest with a pretty bit of greenery in her beak.

She remains inside the nest for quite a while. I begin to think that the man bird will go away disappointed this time, or will sit on the branch of a tree and wait for her as before. But no. Instead, he flies towards the nest, and perches on a twig near it that juts out from the creeper. He looks around a bit. And then he, too, flies inside her nest. I think that there will be a scuffle between them now in there, with loud screeches. I wait for the noise.

But nothing of the kind happens. Peace reigns in the nest. I cannot understand what kind of signal conveyed the woman bird's feelings to him. They share no language to express their feelings. The man bird has understood some subtle signal, and has entered the nest without hesitation, assured of the woman's company.

We humans have verbal intercourse through languages made up of words and sentences. But the sense conveyed by that language becomes contrary to what is intended. Will we be able to find the actual meaning of a wordless language conveyed through gestures and signals? Have I not understood even your wordless signal?

You must be quite fed up by now. Instead of telling you a story, here am I babbling on with all this twaddle. Before you accuse me of doing so, let me tell you something. I have fashioned an escape route for myself. I have cleared that path in the first paragraph itself. If you ask me what drivel is this that I've been spouting all this while, I will retort, why have you assumed that all that I have told you is about myself? I am only telling you a story. The action that the subject of a sentence enacts through the verb, or the significance through which it clears the path ahead, is not controlled by the writer. Notice the way I am immersed as a writer in the liberty of this kind of abdication of responsibility. What a fantastic wall is this, which has been erected by words, in such a manner that reality cannot touch the imaginary. All stories are imaginary. How wonderful! Nobody can touch me if I say that the story that I have told you is imaginary.

But even then the editor may ask, what kind of a romantic story is this? I shall reply, if all romantic imaginings have spontaneous expressions, where does romantic irony come from?

Why Yudhisthir's Story Cannot Be Told

The Yudhisthir I want to tell you about is not the Yudhisthir that everybody knows about. That other Yudhisthir has in the meantime played out his role in the epic, and has gone honourably heavenwards.

There are crores of people who are like the Yudhisthir I am going to tell you about. Even if all the stories ever written in this world were to be added up, there would not be crores of fictional characters. Each one of those crores of people is likely to have individual, distinctive characteristics of his or her own. But it is not very likely that fiction writers will be able to use each one of those characters as raw material for their stories. It is not for this reason that I say that Yudhisthir's story cannot be told.

Of course, before explaining why Yudhisthir's story cannot be written down, a few things must be said about Yudhisthir. Those are the things that I want to tell you.

It cannot be said that absolutely no interesting incidents occurred in Yudhisthir's life. On the other hand, these incidents were not so startling that they could be made delectable with delicious descriptions. These days, almost every day, newspapers publish many juicy stories that wear the garb of truth.

As soon as I utter the words 'garb of truth', I feel like recounting the story about Yudhisthir's name. The Yudhisthir of the epic was a heroic devotee of Truth. The reason behind our Yudhisthir getting his name was also Truth. Not, however, the pursuit of Truth.

Truth, but not the pursuit of Truth. Certainly, a story can be found here if this riddle is solved. Let us proceed.

The first amazing thing that needs to be said is that Yudhisthir's name is not Yudhisthir at all. But now, if enquiries are made about his real name, he himself will either not be able to recall it clearly, or will be unwilling to disclose it. He did have a given name. Since that name has entered the depths of oblivion, there is no point in bringing it back to the light of recollection. But come, let us begin at the beginning. That beginning, though, is not exactly a riveting story.

Before he became Yudhisthir, this was a child born into the unremarkable life of the family of an ordinary farmer in an undistinguished village. The only remarkable thing about his childhood was that he had the opportunity to set foot within the portals of a school, against the wishes of his father, to fulfil his mother's heart's desire. The son of a rustic father would turn out a farmer, too, so where was the need to study? It was with a belief of this kind that the man wished to take his son along with him to the fields as soon as he grew up a little. His unlettered mother was also a farmer's daughter. But she had seen a boy from her family going to college, and, later, going on to the city to work. She had seen him come home occasionally, wearing clothes of sparkling white, riding a shiny bicycle whose bell he kept ringing, and she had breathed the city aroma that clung to him. It was the ambition of the mother, therefore, that her son, too, should study and get a job in the city. It was for this reason that she nagged Yudhisthir's father into making arrangements for sending her son to the village school.

I feel a little uncomfortable about referring to Yudhisthir by this name before he actually became Yudhisthir. Since his real name has vanished, let us call him Nokul for the time being.

Our Nokul showed some inclination for study. Perhaps it was due to his mother's influence. However, the poor boy's intelligence was far from acute. Still, it was not as though he did not climb about three years of classes in the school's scholastic ladder. Perhaps it was due to his mother's influence also that our Nokul was meek and mild. He could not acquire the idle habits of his contemporaries and friends, and tried to do what was required of him at school quite sincerely.

And just for that reason disaster struck.

The schoolteacher did not merely teach, he also had a domestic establishment. What with having to till his fields, and tether his cows and goats, it would be late by the time he reached school. He would be tired, too. Therefore, the teacher would catch up on his lost sleep while he made the class loudly recite either the arithmetic tables, or verses, in the name of study.

Sometimes, he snored as well. He did not pay any attention to what the boys were reciting. It was only after he had had his forty winks that he would wake up with a start, and after teaching one or two lessons, close the school for the day. He would bring with him to the school the cane that as a farmer he used on his cattle while ploughing, and use it liberally on the students if they became too noisy or naughty. The teacher's anger was like a cobra. Sometimes, he would give vent to the anger roused by one boy on another. If a domestic matter had made him angry, he would vent that in the school as well. The boys could sense by his very footsteps that his ire had been roused for some reason at home. On the days this happened, even the naughty ones kept quiet.

That day, the teacher's footsteps did not thud loudly outside the door of the schoolroom. That meant that the teacher was not in an angry state of mind. He came in with a heavy tread, dragging his sandals. He was tired from his work at home that morning. The naughty ones noticed that there was even some mud sticking to the part of their teacher's ankle visible under his dhoti. This meant that he had come straight from the fields to school. There had not even been time to wash up before hurrying here. As soon as he arrived, he gathered the various classes into one large group, and telling the eldest among the students to recite the tables, ordered the others to repeat them after him. After this, he began his nap at his table.

The boys recited their tables, and, growing restive, exchanged impish looks. I do not know who noticed it first, it must have been one of the naughty ones, but they saw that with his mouth open, their teacher was fast asleep, and the folds of his dhoti had come loose. The nudge from the boy who first noticed this made the boy next to him heed it, too. His nudge made another aware, after him, yet another, till the whole school noticed it. After this came the giggles, interspersed with the recitation of the tables. Giggle, giggle, giggle, tables, giggle, giggle, giggle, giggle, tables. This soon became the sound of many voices laughing out loud together, for nobody could control their giggles any more.

The teacher woke up. His had been in a deep sleep. On top of that, as soon as he woke up, he saw that the boys, instead of reciting their tables, were nudging each other and laughing. It was a scene of anarchy. The cobra-like anger was roused at once. He slapped his cane on the table. He stood up with a roar. The boy on whom his eyes fell still had a laugh pasted on his sharp face. Even though others, too, had the same, it was this boy's laugh that the teacher noticed immediately. Looking at him, the teacher roared, 'Hey, you mongoose, what are you laughing about? Why are you making such a noise, ha?' Saying this, the teacher advanced towards the boy.

The boy was meek and mild, the Nokul or Yudhisthir of our story. But the contagion of laughter had touched him, as well. When the others were all laughing, how could he keep from doing so? The teacher never remembered any boy's name, and indeed, never thought it necessary to do so at all. He addressed each boy according to requirement and occasion. When his eyes fell on this boy's face, he whirled his cane in the air and began to advance towards him. His dhoti was already open. Its folds had come undone, and it was dragging on the floor. But he remained unaware of this. Even at that time, the mischief-makers in the back rows continued to giggle, but instead of acting on that, the angry teacher went to the lad standing on the bamboo mat, and asked in a thunderous voice, 'Hey, what are you sniggering at, you brat?' He whirled his cane mightily. Mamma's boy that he was, the lad remembered his mother's teaching, 'Always speak the truth', and pointing to his teacher's dhoti, said, 'Sir, sir, dhoti…' It was only then that the teacher noticed his dhoti, with its folds undone. Instead of getting embarrassed at his own carelessness, he directed his anger at the boy who had caught him unawares by pointing out the truth.

Slashing at the boy's back with his cane, he said, 'Have you come here to study, or to gape at other people's dhotis, you mongoose?' In order to manage his dhoti, he dismissed the entire school for the day.

The boy's schoolfellows laughed shrilly at him, teasing him by calling him 'Mongoose! Mongoose!' halfway down the road home. He had no objection to assuming the name of Mongoose, any name was good enough for others to call him by. What he did not understand was why the cane had whizzed down on him. Swallowing this first injury that came his way for telling the truth, he reached home.

It is not for nothing that we have temporarily given our Nokul this particular name. After this incident, his peers kept calling him 'Mongoose! Oi mongoose!' This continued until the teacher bestowed somebody else with another name.

The second crisis was even more serious. After our Nokul was promoted to the next class, his father, giving in to his mother's nagging, bought him a new slate. On the very first day that he came to school with the new slate, some rascal's gaze fell on it. This rogue's own slate was broken. He could not mention it at home because he himself had broken it. But he definitely needed a good slate. Therefore, as soon as he noticed our Nokul's new slate, a ploy for appropriating it came to his mind.

Before entering the classroom, the boys of the school would keep their slates, pencils, books and the mats of split bamboo on which they sat, on the veranda, and go to the tube-well nearby to take a drink of water. That day, our Nokul, too, kept his new slate in this manner, and went to have a drink of water. The rascal placed his own broken slate and books beneath Nokul's, and, as soon as Nokul returned from the water pump, confronted him, 'Oi, you've put your slate on top of mine. You've broken my slate.' Nokul had already seen the rascal's broken slate before this. He therefore protested vehemently. He had never kept his own slate on top of that rogue's, and in any case that slate was already broken. The rascal's friends, too, were rogues. They added their voices in chorus to their friend's, 'No, no, you've broken it, you've broken it! We saw it!'

The teacher appeared. The rascal tattled, 'Sir, he's broken my slate!'

The teacher asked, 'Hey, did you break his slate?'

Nokul spoke truthfully, 'No, I did not break it, his slate was already broken.'

The rascal's friends began to shriek, 'He broke it, we saw him!'

The teacher asked again, 'Oi, why don't you tell the truth, did you break it or not?'

Once more, he replied, 'No, sir, I did not.'

Once more the rogues shouted their denial in chorus.

The teacher's verdict: 'Hu, Dharmaveer Yudhisthir, Truth-Teller, he's not broken it. Not broken it, indeed. You've broken it all right. Go on, give him your slate, and you take his broken one.' The teacher continued mockingly, 'Dharmaveer, go home and tell your father to buy you a new one.'

This time, even though the teacher did not cane him on his back, a slash landed on Nokul's mind. In addition, he had lost his new slate, and after school finished, the rascals jeered at him, calling him 'Yudhisthir! Yudhisthir!'

When he showed his broken slate and told the truth at home, even his father thought that he himself had broken the new slate, and was now telling a lie. He was rewarded by his father with a box on his cheek.

In school, he began to be called 'Yudhisthir,' first by

the rascals, then by all the others. As his peers used this name continuously, it became settled that it was indeed his name. Later, he himself came to assume that this was his actual name. His parents, of course, kept calling him by his given name.

An important fact will remain untold if the reason for Yudhisthir having to leave school is not given here. The scoundrels of the school would frequently indulge in all kinds of hooliganism, and quite often, like a person venting the anger roused by bed bugs onto the ragged mat of split bamboo, the teacher's wrath would fall on the boys who were meek and mild. During the days when the fields had to be ploughed, he would be more tired.

It was on one such day that a wicked plan occurred to the rascals of the school. They wished to put some stinging nettle on the teacher's desk, and then watch the fun. One day, before the rest of the school arrived, the rascals put the nettle leaves on the teacher's desk. For some reason, Yudhisthir had reached school early that day. He witnessed this deed of theirs. The scoundrels warned him, 'We won't spare you if you tattle on us.'

The teacher arrived, and, as was his habit, gave the boys a poem to recite. Placing his hands on the table, he was about to lower his head, when the sting of the nettles started an unbearable itch on his hands and head. The more he scratched, the worse the itch became. In the meantime, there were whispers and suppressed chortles coming from the back rows.

Those in the front rows were in dire straits, for they,

too, felt like bursting out laughing. Their faces were contorted with the effort to hold their laughter in. The teacher suspected that this was the handiwork of one of this lot. He would scratch himself, then look suspiciously at each face, hoping to catch the culprit out. As soon as his glance fell on them, the suppressed whispers would stop, the boys would swallow their giggles, and their bodies would shake with repressed mirth. The teacher, scratching his face and body uncontrollably with both hands, advanced threateningly towards the boys. He would not let off the scoundrels who had placed the nettles on his table easily.

It was Yudhisthir's bad luck. Those eyes, inflamed with fury, fell straightaway on him, even though there was no reason to suspect him. However, he was sitting in the first row. He was innocent, so what was there to be frightened of, he had thought, and had not even laughed. But the very fact of his not laughing became the reason for suspicion, and the teacher asked, 'Ei, Dharmaveer, who kept this stuff on the table? What was it? You're sitting there so primly, was it you who kept it?'

From behind, the rascals shouted in a highly enthusiastic chorus, 'Sir, it's him, sir! He's the one who put the nettles there,' and so on. No matter how strenuously the boy said, 'No, I didn't put them there,' the chorus would increase in strength. Eventually, fed up, and forgetting, in his bid to save his own skin, the warning that the rascals had given him earlier, he screeched, 'I didn't put it there, sir. Those fellows did it.' Saying this, he pointed at the rascals.

The volume of the scoundrels' chorus rose even higher. 'He's a lying Yudhisthir, sir. He put it there. We saw him. And now he's blaming us.'

Standing before Yudhisthir, the teacher's anger increased in proportion to the increase in his itch. Unable to decide who had placed the nettles there, he decided the matter according to his own judgement by walloping Yudhisthir's back mercilessly with his cane, saying 'So, you've become Yudhisthir!' It was only after this that he felt some relief from the itchiness. Having no patience left to continue teaching, he declared school over for the day, and rushed home.

Yudhisthir, too, returned home along with the other boys, moaning with the pain of the slashes from the teacher's cane on his back. The jeers of the rascals, who kept calling out, 'Oi Yudhisthir, Oi Yudhsithir' all the way back only increased the pain.

After this, despite all her pleas and pleadings, Yudhisthir's mother failed to get him to return to school. Not only did he not go to school ever again, in his own mind, he took a tremendous oath. From that day, he decided that he would never speak the truth again. He mastered the habit of telling glib lies so well that he was even able to believe the untruth to be the truth. If the telling of a truth led to such problems in life, then why should he tell it? This became his philosophy of life.

After this, when we meet him again, he is a boatman. In spite of all his efforts, his father could not turn him towards the fields. Seeing an affinity for boats in his son, who by then was loafing around aimlessly, his father sent him with his own boat to the ghat by the river, hoping that this would steady him. And steady him it did.

His mother had wished her son to be an educated, urban dweller. Yudhisthir hardly had any schooling, and could never go to the city. But the ghat where he became a ghatoi, a ferryman, pleased him. He stayed on at that place. Gradually, shops and other establishments appeared around that ghat. An open-air marketplace, too, sprang up there. The number of people who crossed the river increased. A police outpost was established some distance away. In this manner, an aroma of the city came to Ghatoi Yudhisthir. His mother's wish came true, even if in a roundabout manner. Later, finding it difficult to commute from home, Yudhisthir built a small hut on the banks of the river. And people, too, found it convenient when the ferryman began to stay overnight at the ghat itself.

Yudhisthir faced no problem whatsoever during the times when he lied so glibly. But what kind of a story has no incident, no problem, no strife, where life moves in uncomplicated lines? There is none of that in this portion of Yudhisthir's life. But it is not for this reason that I say that Yudhisthir's story cannot be told.

He is not the hero of some delectable tale. But the story of how he became entangled in this tale needs to be told. We shall try to search out the wellspring of that story.

Incidents do not make up a story. A story is created when a problem arises in the plot, which gives a twist to the tale. But let me give you the preface.

Speaking the truth during his childhood had proved disastrous for Yudhisthir. After this, without any further calamity, he became a teenager. Gradually, he became a youth. And after that, he became the ferryman who was known to all. People from the town knew him, people from the village knew him. Ploughmen knew him, traders knew him. Thieves knew him, the police knew him. They all knew him, because everybody crossed the river on his boat. By now, everybody knew that he was a glib liar. Since his lies did not harm anybody, nobody was bothered. The daroga of the thana also knew that he was a habitual liar. Let me tell you the rather appetising story of how the daroga came to know this.

One day, soon after his transfer to this place, in the course of conducting an investigation, the daroga had had to catch a boat to cross the river. Sitting in the boat, the daroga struck up a conversation with the ferryman. At that time, the daroga did not know the ferryman's name. He asked, 'So, Ghatoi, what's your name?'

'Yudhisthir, sir.' The ferryman was not about to tell the daroga his real name, and thus disclose the truth.

The daroga joked, 'Aah, here's a Dharmaveer!'

He had replied, 'Dharma is my father's name.'

The daroga indeed thought his father's name to be Dharma. Once more, he asked, 'Is that so? Where does your father live?'

'Deuta is on the other shore, Master.'

The daroga had assumed that the father had passed away, or gone on to the shores of eternity.

It was in this way that Yudhisthir had fun, by spicing up his mendacious words in conversation. Yudhisthir's father's name was not Dharma. He meant he believed in Dharma, or Virtue. (He had in the meantime accepted the art of lying to be a virtue.) Besides, Yudhisthir's father had not died. Yudhisthir's village, where his father lived, was on the other bank of the river. It was only much later that the daroga was able to make out the true meaning of Yudhisthir's cryptic language. He was wonderstruck at Yudhisthir's expertise in speaking in this manner.

If he had not been wonderstruck, Yudhisthir would not have entered this story at all. The straight line of his life would have moved like the thread on a loom, from this bank of the river to the other.

How can Yudhisthir's life remain without incident? I have already said that a small town had sprung up around the ghat. Of course there was still a scent of the rural about the place. In the village, rumours fly thick and fast. In the town an incident creates an uproar. Since the place where Yudhisthir's ghat was situated was halfway to being a town, both incident and rumour occurred there. There was grist for rumourmongers, but since it was a small town, the gossip resonated all around, and became a topic for discussion among the people.

A variety of passengers crossed the river on Yudhisthir's boat. When some incident occurred, there would be heated discussions among the passengers on his boat. However, he did not take much part in them. Some of the passengers were known to him, some unknown.

Sometimes, he would let loose a falsehood in the conversation of those he knew, and put the heat on the topic under discussion. The people whom he knew were those who crossed the river daily. It was because they did so every day that he remembered their faces.

However, one day, a couple of faces that he saw remained in his memory. An unknown youth crossed the river with a young girl very early one morning. The young man returned in the evening. The young girl did not accompany him back. It was dusk. There was no need for Yudhisthir to look attentively at the youth. But the young man, after sitting down in the boat, asked Yudhisthir, 'Ghatoi, do you see me?'

This was a senseless question. Yudhisthir could see the youth in front of him, and yet here was the young man asking if Yudhisthir could see him! Yudhisthir therefore took a good look at him. Of course a reply quickly tripped off his tongue, used as it was to lying smoothly, 'No, I don't see you, deo.'

The youth said approvingly, 'Good, good, you haven't seen me.' After that, he changed his tone, and threatened, 'But listen now. Even if someone asks you, tell them you haven't seen me.'

It was a very simple calculation for Yudhisthir. He smelled something fishy at this threat. But he could recite the tables of untruth very fluently. Therefore, it did not take Yudhisthir even a moment to nod his head.

In the town, though, an incident occurred which stunned the daroga. Since the elections were round the corner, the rumour mills, too, became busy at the same time. The incident had the potential of putting the government in a spot. The dead body of a young girl was discovered in a thickly wooded place. The girl had been pregnant.

It was a serious affair. There were demands that the culprit should be brought to book immediately. The Opposition said the ruling party should be ashamed, the law and order situation was going to the dogs. The ruling party was in danger of losing the coming elections. The daroga was spending sleepless nights. The order from the top was inflexible. The murderer had to be nabbed quickly. Otherwise, the daroga would not be able to hang on to his job.

Everybody grew highly agitated, not because of the pitiful end of the girl, but because of the political rumours. The daroga would be in trouble if he could not handle the situation. But after prostrating himself full length at the temple of Bholanath the Saviour, a ray of divine illumination came to him. The inquiry began to move on the path of a speedy conclusion. Very soon, the culprit was arrested.

The criminal was thus discovered. But where were the statements from the witnesses? Without a statement from a witness, how could the daroga produce the accused in the wooden enclosure of the courtroom?

It was then that the daroga remembered Yudhisthir. Through the junior daroga, he issued a summons and had Yudhisthir brought to the thana. The daroga told Yudhisthir, 'You will have to be a witness.'

Yudhisthir was dumbfounded. It seemed as though the thread on his loom was getting all tangled up. 'Witness, hujoor, I?'

'Yes, you. Don't worry. The murderer has been nabbed. All you have to do is say that you recognize him.'

The thread on his loom appeared to shuttle swiftly before Yudhisthir's eyes. Wrapped in the scandal of much rumour, this piquant affair had become a story running into several instalments among the passengers travelling on his boat. Since he was past master at fabricating untruths, Yudhisthir would occasionally add a bit of colour to the scandal, stirring up the stories told by his passengers. That was all. And now here was the daroga, catching him and bringing him to this place to become a witness.

He asked fearfully, 'What will I have to say, hujoor?'

The daroga replied, 'You will have to say that you know who the murderer is. You have seen him killing the victim.'

This meant that he would not have to tell the truth. Fabrications came easily to him. Yudhisthir had not seen the murder take place. He drew a breath of relief. He was always ready to fib. He said, 'All right, hujoor.'

The daroga told him, 'Make sure you say everything properly. I will tell you what you have to say. I will give you a reward if you stand witness properly.'

Yudhisthir already knew that telling the truth led to punishment. Now, he realized that telling an untruth brought rewards.

The daroga said, 'The murderer is already in the

lockup. I will present you in court in advance. The lawyer will question you. Say that you recognize the man. I will tell you how the incident happened. Tell them exactly what I teach you. There'll be a reward for you, and for me, too. But if there's the slightest discrepancy, you will go right off to the other shore.'

'The other shore' did not mean the shores of eternity, after death. What the daroga meant was that Yudhisthir would have to leave the ghat and return to his father's village, and sit idle and empty-handed in the barren fields. The daroga had used the words 'other shore' from Yudhisthir's own earlier phrase. But Yudhisthir was not worried. After all, he would just have to recite some lies. He was an expert at cooking up falsehoods, which sputtered out from his mouth like freshly popped puffed rice.

In due course, Yudhisthir appeared in the court. The daroga had coached him on what he was to say. He had also secretly shown Yudhisthir the accused in the lockup. The imprisoned man was not unknown to him. He was a thief. He had occasionally crossed the river on his boat. But what was it to Yudhisthir, anyway? He would have to take an oath, then tell the untruth. He would recite the untruth quite merrily. When the daroga coached him on how to speak as a witness, he also showed Yudhisthir a picture of the dead girl. It was only when he saw the picture that he was startled. She had crossed the river on his boat just once. But he still remembered her. She had gone to the other bank, and not returned. Her corpse had turned up the next day.

The courtroom. The accused was in the wooden enclosure. Yudhisthir was the eyewitness. The judge was in his seat. Yudhisthir had already taken an oath to speak the truth, and he would then tell untruths. The Government pleader was getting ready to present the case. Before replying to the lawyer's questions, Yudhisthir, seeking reassurance from the daroga, looked around to see where he was sitting, and glanced at the people in the front row.

Yudhisthir's heart leaped mightily within him. There, no doubt was the daroga sitting there with a reassuring look on his face. But who was that with him? Yudhisthir had seen the plump-faced person sitting right next to the daroga countless times on the election posters, his smiling visage waving gently in the breeze. He was seeking the votes of the public again for re-election in the coming polls. A young man sat beside him. Yudhisthir recognized him. He had crossed the river on his boat very early one morning with the young girl. The youth had returned alone in the evening. He had warned Yudhisthir not to tell anyone that he had seen him. The girl's corpse had turned up the next day. Yudhisthir did not know what a montage was. But the three or four scenes that flashed before his eyes were like the montage in a film. Even if the others in this courtroom did not know who the actual murderer was, Yudhisthir was now sure about his identity. That youth was the murderer. He was sitting near his powerful father with a wide grin on his face.

Ferryman Yudhishtir had set out to tell a simple story with his fib. But now his craft had run aground on the sands of the river's edge. The yarn of the story was entangled in the twisting-reel of his falsehood.

That, which was just a yarn, becomes a story at this point. I want to tell you this story about Yudhisthir. How can Yudhisthir solve this problem? The story will conclude only when the yarn is unknotted.

Yudhisthir knew the thief who was standing, bewildered, in the wooden enclosure. Would he now lie to the honourable court and point out the thief to be the murderer? His evidence could send the man to the gallows.

In that case, in this breathless moment, would he then, bruised and battered by his wounded conscience, become upright and truthful? Would he then point a finger to the young man, and say, 'Honourable Judge, that young man is the murderer. It's him you must try.'

It is quite possible for the story to unravel in this manner. This solution has been dramatically shown innumerable times on the silver screen to the enthusiastic applause of the audience.

The writer is prepared to accept this solution as a means of unkotting the yarn.

But...

In his mind's eye, Yudhisthir equated the young man and his stout father with his old schoolteacher. The folds of his dhoti were open, in his hand was the cane used by ploughmen to beat the cows.

Yudhisthir was stunned. The cane was moving to and fro. His story had got stuck at that point.

Even then, the writer wishes to take the story forward. It doesn't matter that problems are created in stories, they are closed within the story, too. It is only then that the story is completed.

But the writer's pen remains stuck.

Certainly you should be told the reason for this. An example will have to be given. Since you, too, were once the editor of a newspaper, I wish to give you this particular example.

Take, for instance, a particular newspaper. Thousands of copies are sold, the paper's popularity rises enormously. But the readers know that those luscious news items that are published every day contain no truth. And this is why they read it. They read it because it is fiction. A story.

Would readers believe it if that newspaper were to publish a truth?

In that case…

If Yudhisthir, who had always lied so glibly, if he were to point to the murderer and tell the truth, would anybody believe it to be the truth? Yudhisthir's story cannot move beyond this question.

The writer is helpless. The writer has no idea where the convolutions of the story will lead. The temperature of the flame beneath the vessel of the story has risen high. But the story is yet to be cooked through.

The Bestower of Death

I met the young man on the sixtieth anniversary of my birth. I was quite well acquainted with those devoted readers of mine who had organized the diamond jubilee celebrations of my birth, and this restless young man was not one of them. He came forward when the function ended. He said, 'I wish to interview you.' I agreed immediately. I liked being in the limelight, and these jubilee celebrations organized by my loyal admirers had filled me with satisfaction.

But the young man's very first question was unusual, and I was a little taken aback. He asked me, 'Are you afraid of death?' Such an unhappy question on such a happy day! But I did not wish to complain. I replied, 'No. I am not afraid of death. I will die one day in any case.'

The answer was a lie. But I made it credible with a dazzling smile. Actually, before the young man had asked me that question, I had not given any thought to my own death. But I had become aware of it as soon as he had uttered the words 'afraid of death,' and a fear had indeed sprung up in my mind when I realized that I too would be dead one day. I felt that today's celebration of my birthday was a kind of precursor to the obsequies after my death. It occurred to me that this celebration was organized only to mark the fact that we were nearer to my death by a year.

The young man's second question was even stranger. 'Do you consider death to be fated?'

At first, I did not understand the question. I asked, 'Meaning…?'

He said, 'For instance, you may fall ill and die due to a wrong line of treatment. Or you can step out of the house and die in a car accident. You may be struck down by an unskilled driver, or exterminated by a killer. Do you still believe that we only live the number of days that are pre-ordained by God, and that humans have nothing to do with death?'

I was happy at his question. I believe that nobody can snatch away the allotted days of a person's life from him. Nobody can die unless it is fated. I replied accordingly. Without saying anything, the young man only laughed. I did not understand the significance of his laughter.

His third question: 'The stories that you write are pleasant and engrossing. Just by looking at the large number of your fans, one can make out that you are a very popular writer. There are so many of your eager fans gathered here at this celebratory function today. My question is, do you write to keep your admiring readers happy, and feed their imaginations with delicious, satisfying fare? Or do you search for some significance in the numerous incidents that take place all around us? Do your writings reflect reality?'

I did not care for the question. I hope for praise from my readers. Therefore I write what the majority of my readers enjoy. Why should I write otherwise? How could I have become such a popular writer unless I catered to what my readers wanted? What is the role of words such as 'significance' and 'reality' in all of this?

I replied, 'Look, if people enjoy reading what I write, then my success lies in that. That itself is the significance of my writings. The barometer of my writing lies in the delight and the taste of my readers. They look for pleasing stories, and that is what I give them.'

I noticed that the youth nodded. However, I could not make out if he nodded in agreement with my words, or due to some other reason. He asked me many more questions of various kinds. One of his questions seemed to be a kind of riddle. In fact, it would be more appropriate to call it a statement rather than a question. He asked, 'Do you believe that people die twice? One is of course the physical death. As soon as a person stops breathing, he is dead. There is also a societal death. For example: a writer's popularity comes to an end. He has no readers, he is forgotten. That is his societal death.'

He remained silent for a while after this speech. Presently, he asked, 'Do you believe in the existence of this kind of death?'

I was baffled by his question. I looked at my committed admirers, who still surrounded me. Was it possible that they could forget me? And even if they did forget me, why should I die? I had already got what I needed by then, especially fame and money. I was in good shape, physically. I believed that I would live a full and complete life. After living successfully and satisfactorily, one day I would die. That would be my only death. Why would I die before that? I told the young man as much. I noticed that the youth was in the habit of nodding. It was somewhat irritating. But I did not tell him my opinion on his habit.

He asked his final question before taking his leave. He said, 'Look here, all those who have spoken today have wished you a long life, a hundred years of life, even. But how long do you yourself think you will live?'

Without thinking, I responded, 'Ninety years. Got it? Ninety years.' Even as I said it, I realized that the answer was somewhat ridiculous. Why did I say 'ninety years' in that manner?

A few days ago, I had met a ninety-year-old person whom I had, till then, mistakenly assumed to be dead, sitting at a function in a healthy physical state and happy frame of mind. Perhaps it was for that reason that the words 'ninety years' had come to me in a flash like that. I too was in good health. I did not suffer from any disease or ailment. Besides, the teeming presence of my numerous fans gave me a sense of security with regard to my writing. The prospect of sudden death did not even enter my mind.

What was it that happened, normally, during

interviews? The interviewer asked a few questions, and I, in turn, gave whatever answers came to my mind. Later, I thought of neither the question nor the answer. I was quite happy if my reply could amaze my loyal readers. Just as the tastes of my readers flavoured my writings, my name, too, was immortalized through their pleasure. As a writer, I felt a sense of completeness, of wholeness, with this. The rest was irrelevant.

But the young man's questions seemed to have pierced my contentment in some places. These strange queries had tangled up my well-ordered mind. I kept thinking of them, repeatedly. I began to realize, vaguely, that the literary web that I wove was a latticework of the imagination.

This net did not catch the answers to questions based on reality, for it was not being cast in the pool of actuality. The louder the enthusiastic applause of fans, the more reality became unreal.

Perhaps these tangled thoughts would have been erased in time. But then, the biggest bomb blast that our town has ever seen happened that very day. Looking at the pictures in the newspapers that showed the grotesquely-scattered body parts, I was revolted. I created in my stories an agreeable world, where beautiful characters spoke brilliantly, where love and affection, feelings and sentiments and many other elements made the story attractive, where numerous enthusiastic readers found delectable fare. This terrible happening seemed to have twisted my beautiful world of the imagination, and turned it on its head. Was the incident itself false, or was the beautiful world of my creation a sham?

Why was I getting these delusions? There had been explosions earlier as well. Numerous violent incidents had been reported in the papers. But, engrossed as I had been in creating stories that would touch the hearts of my adoring readers, I had never been moved by them. I was bewildered today, for I recognized the face that belonged to the scattered remnants of the body. Tangled around it was my reply to the question asked by the smart young man at the diamond jubilee celebrations. I had said that death was in the hands of Fate. Did Fate use this shattered body as a sacrificial offering in this explosion?

I am now ninety years old. I am lying on the bed as though I am pasted to it, as I wait for death. Actually, I wish to welcome death with enthusiasm. My memory is failing. I do not recognize the faces of those people who come with curiosity to see me. Sometimes, a grey-haired person, about sixty years old, comes and sits near me. He greets me gently, 'Deuta'. I keep staring at the man's face, but I do not recognize him. He asks me, 'How are you?' I find the question meaningless. Suspended between Being and Non-Being, I feel no fear.

I feel it is normal to Not Be, and I understand that after enjoying a full life, what remains is only the event of Not Being. I wait with a great deal of satisfaction for that moment when Fate will call me.

As soon as I think of the word Fate, I remember the fine-looking face of that smart and intelligent young man. I remember also, very clearly, those questions that he had asked me on my sixtieth birth anniversary. My memory is failing. I do not know how the person who sits by my side every day is related to me, he who calls me 'Deuta', Father, holds my hand and asks me some questions, even if I try to give my memory a shake. But those questions that the young man had asked that day, and his face, have remained indelibly imprinted on my memory. He was clever, that boy. It occurs to me now that there was a dissonance between two of his questions, and my replies. To one of his questions, I had replied that a person's death was pre-ordained. And yet, in reply to his question about the age at which I would die, I had said that I would live till ninety. Instead of allowing Fate to decide on it, I myself had made a decision. I remember the way he had smiled on hearing this. Now, in the moments preceding my death, I understand the meaning of that smile.

But I really am about to die at the age of ninety. My destiny has given me this span of life. If he had been around at this moment, I would have told that young man, 'Look, Fate has given me this lifespan. I am now listlessly preparing to die. Those people who come to my room to look at me with curiosity are also, doubtless, waiting for the moment of my death. I sometimes see a middle-aged woman along with that elderly man who calls me Deuta. Every now and again, a lively child looks in on me with curiosity. It seems that she is the granddaughter of that elderly man and the middle-aged woman. A young woman comes in sometimes, and addresses me as Koka. Grandfather. It seems she is the mother of that vivacious little child. When I think of these relationships, I am confused. Just a while ago, an old woman of about eighty or eighty-one came and sat by me. She remained looking at my face very eagerly. I do not understand what she had been looking for. She has come before to this room, as well. Today, as soon as she sits by me, I ask her, for courtesy's sake, 'I hope you are well? When did you come to Guwahati?' I gasp out the words.

Possibly, I will lose my voice in a while. I hear some kind of rattle in my throat. My question appears to startle the old woman. Without saying anything, she walks out of the room with an unsteady gait. I hear her telling the elderly man outside the room, 'Your Deuta doesn't recognize me.'

The man enters the room, and says, 'Deuta, that's Ma.'

I fail to understand what their relationship has to do with me. I am not going to go into such complex matters now. I say, without much thought, 'OK'.

Actually, I am waiting to die. I have no kind of apprehension. I do not recognize these people who come near me and address me by a relationship term. I see on their faces signs of anxiety. Not because I will die, for they know that I am dying. I hear them whispering about the things that will be needed for the rituals and obsequies after I am dead. Perhaps their anxiety is because they do not know the exact moment when death will claim me. They take turns to come and keep vigil by my side. I want to tell them that there is no need to watch over me. After all, I am not afraid! Truly, I feel no fear at all as I wait for the last moment of my life. I know now that I had not lied to that young questioner on the occasion of my sixtieth birthday. I do not fear death.

Once more, I remember the young man's face. There was no opportunity to meet up with him again. But why do I have such a clear memory of his face? Is it because he had asked some strange questions to a writer, one who took life to be an exciting story, simply told?

Why, I do not recognize even those people who live in this house, whom I meet every day. Even their connections to me are confusing. And yet I remember the likeness of that young man so clearly.

He had asked me another question, hadn't he? Something about a person dying twice. One was a physical death, and the other, societal. He had asked me: if, suppose, a writer like me was to be erased from the collective memory, would it be a societal death or not? Hadn't I told him then that people only died once? But that question had disturbed me. Looking that day at those who had organized my birthday celebrations, and the audience at that function, I had thought that I would always remain alive in their minds. In fact, they would keep my name alive even after I died. I had thought that people could achieve immortality in this manner through their achievements even after their physical death. Even so, I had been confused. Hadn't I thought then that if my readers were to forget me, my societal death might indeed occur? I had been popular among them only because I knew what kind of fare was needed for their mental gratification. What if their tastes changed? Even though I had tried to ignore thoughts of this nature, I had not been able to keep them away from my mind.

When I was about seventy-five or so, I had realized that I was not being read by newer readers. My writing too had stopped, for the wellsprings of my imagination had dried up. Once, I had seen a newspaper article where the word 'Late' was prefixed to my name. This meant that I had already vanished from public memory. Even so, I had not been concerned. To begin with, I had become indifferent to writing. But I had also lost my desire for immortality. Had the young man been indicating this, then? Was the disappearance of this desire also a kind of death? My physical death at a mature age is going to be my second death, merely. Do I finally understand the great significance underlying the young man's questions now, at ninety, as I count the final moments till my death?

I had told the young man that I was not afraid of death. But in the deepest recesses of my mind, perhaps a fear of Death had indeed been born at that point. Why had I shivered at the picture of the effects of the bomb explosion—the pieces of human bodies flung grossly in all directions? Was it only because of the extreme brutality of the incident? The result was that because of this block to the effortless flowing stream of my imagination, I could not match this world to the pleasant universe that I created in my stories, those tales that thrilled my faithful readers who waited with impatient enthusiasm for my next story.

It was from that time that I had gradually become unable to write. Large clumps of floating vegetation began to block the hitherto free-flowing stream of my imagination. I began to feel as though my pen was only creating meaningless squiggles. At the age of seventy-five, I had seen the word 'Late' prefixed to my name, but as a writer, hadn't I already faced the jaws of death even before that? Had a fear of death been born in me at that time, a fear that I had not understood then?

I understand now why I had shivered at that moment. I had not wanted a gruesome death like that for myself. Pictures of previous bomb explosions had not affected me in this way. But the picture of this terrible blast had brought to my mind the possibility of a similarly ghastly death for myself. What then was the difference between this explosion and previous ones? There was indeed a difference. For this one had hit me perceptibly. This explosion had occurred on my sixtieth birth anniversary. And I had recognized the dead body. The corpse was twisted and distorted. Even so, I had thought, the owner of that body, now dead, could very well have been me instead of that young man who had questioned me. In that case, my sixtieth birth anniversary would have been the last day of my life. The young man who had questioned me about death had stepped out from my birthday celebrations and died an unnatural death by being blown to pieces. If my fans had not been surrounding me, I too would have gone out, and then perhaps it would have been I who would have fallen as a sacrifice to the killers.

The incident had happened not too far from the place where the celebrations had been held. The young man must have come face to face with death just after questioning me. It was only the next day, however, that I had been able to recognize the scattered body parts in the newspaper.

After that, my pen had come to a halt. The incident would come to mind, repeatedly, and block my beautiful imaginings. I could not correlate the physical world in which I lived with the charming, attractive world that I created in my stories, and my pen became impotent. I became incapable of creativity. This inability turned into an immense rage. Its very impotence, instead of disturbing me, churned my blocked creative energies to a great anger. Coming out from the latticework of the imagination, I would criticize harshly those who were at the root of this destruction.

My fans would ask, 'What are you doing? Why have you stopped writing your charming stories? The things you write about these days don't go with your beautiful style.'

They did not understand that I was unable to recreate that world which I had shaped earlier. My helplessness had made me so impotent as a writer that I had begun to spout venom against those demonic wrongdoers. It was not as though I had taken up my pen against terror because of some deep-seated ideology. Nor did I regain my lost capacity to write through these noxious outpourings. It was because of this that my prideful rants could create no impression on any reader. I could not create a group of admiring praise-givers through these writings of mine. I stopped writing.

When, at the age of seventy-five, somebody said that I was dead, I was neither irritated nor impatient. I became indifferent to the world, and stopped following the events that took place in it. Perhaps my subconscious mind had embraced this cunning ploy. As a result, I lead an even, tranquil life. And now, at the age of ninety, after enjoying a full life, I am ready to face the moment of my death without any fear. I do not need immortality. I have stopped recognizing people, I do not remember them. Why should others need to recognize and remember me? Had I not wished for a tranquil death, just like this?

But why, at this moment, am I continually remembering that young man whose questions had created such a tumult in me? Why do various implications and connotations of his questions come repeatedly to my mind?

I am now sixty-four years old. I am sitting on my veranda, my wife is at my side. I remember my sixtieth birthday, four years ago. That birthday was celebrated with great fanfare, publicly. None of my fans are by my side today.

My birthday has passed quietly in the company of my wife. During these last four years, I have not been able to write a single story or novel. If I sit down to write, I see in my mind's eye the young man's shattered body parts, and the world that I am trying to create seems false, unreal and strange. In sadness and anger, in these last few years, instead of writing stories, I have been criticizing those terrorists in harsh, angry terms, I have condemned them and compared them to demons and fiends.

Today, sitting on my veranda, I am imagining a beautiful death at the probable age of ninety. What a calm and tranquil death! Yes, on my sixty-fourth birthday, I have created an imaginary story about my approaching death at ninety. This story is not like my previous pleasant tales. This story is not meant for my readers, either. It is only for me. To release my agitations, I have created a peaceful story in my mind about an imaginary death.

I notice that my wife keeps staring at my face at frequent intervals. We have been quiet for a long time. Finally, she looks at me and asks, 'Why is your face looking so pale? Is something wrong?'

I do not say anything. I put my hand in the breast pocket of my shirt and take out from there a piece of paper that someone has thrown into the letter box today. There is a single sentence written there. I have read that sentence many times during the day. There is no name on the paper. There is no need for that. Those who have written it know that I know. A decision has been taken, and the news of the directive has been sent to me: 'You have been awarded the death sentence.'

Just two days ago, I had tried to write a story and failed. I had become furious. The 'baseless statement' that I had made in anger that day, saying that certain people should be publicly hanged, had led to this. Those I had named had now awarded me the death sentence.

My face has no doubt become like a corpse's by now. My wife has said I look pale. I give her the piece of paper. A white piece of paper. Blank. My wife looks at it in astonishment. She then looks up and stares at my face. Forgetting her, I wait for the Bestower of Death to come and execute his sentence.

Post-modern: A Story

Two autorickshaws. There are three of us.

Geographer, Silencer, and I, Poet.

We could have travelled in one auto. But Geographer is a senior person. I'm not sure whether he is actually senior to us in years, but we have accepted him as an elder, even a leader. Therefore, he has the right of a senior to an auto all on his own. In any case, the arrangement is that the fare for both autorickshaws will be divided equally among the three of us.

Each one of us has a suitcase in our hands. It is summer. There is no need for warm clothing or blankets. A bedsheet apiece. Inside our suitcases are inflatable-rubber pillows. For a four-day stay, this is quite enough.

We alight at the railway station full of enthusiasm. Geographer rushes off to examine the Rijarbheson Sart. (That is, 'Reservation Chart'. I prefer to write these words the way I say them. I get highly confused when I see the debates raging in the papers regarding pronunciation. My tongue, used to local foods such as khaar, refuses to say them in the way they are supposed to be in English.)

Since Geographer strides off towards the Rijarbheson Sart with the responsible gait of a senior, both of us, that is, Silencer and Poet, pay off the two autos with the responsibility that devolves on us as younger brothers.

After the autorickshaws depart, Geographer bustles out busily from inside the station, and comes up to where we stand. He makes as though to take his wallet out of his pocket. Looking at us, he says, 'Oh, you've paid them already? Fine. We have got our rijarbhesons. Come on now, it's number seven.' In other words, our train will pull in at Platform Number Seven.

See how hasty writing leads to the omission of many facts? I've yet to tell you the most important thing. We have started out on this train journey with a very laudable aim in mind. We are setting out to attend the annual session of the conference on Asomiya literature. Silencer has only one worry. He is quite a gourmet. He is concerned about the culinary arrangements at the conference. We hear that arrangements have been made to transport a truckload of fish from this place itself. Silencer is satisfied. We, too, are happy. For it is after many years of struggle that, just this year, we have finally managed to obtain recognition for our unit. This is our first trip to the conference as representatives of our unit, our branch of the main literary organization. Of course, Geographer had attended this conference earlier. An intelligent man, he had gone through the good offices of a branch other than our own.

Our literary circle was named 'Progoti Sahitya

Kanon' at the time of its inception. The Progressive Literary Forum. After several years of trying futilely to get recognition from the main literary organization, Geographer's suspicions had been aroused. It had been Geographer who had changed the name to 'Surabhi Sahitya Kanon.' 'The Fragrant Literary Forum,' or even, in the changed context, 'The Fragrant Literary Grove.' Below this was written, in small letters, 'Fearlessly working for the betterment of regional literature.' In no time at all, our forum got its recognition. It should be mentioned, also, that Geographer had done all he could to speed up matters in other ways as well. Indeed, Geographer insisted that the recognition was very much the product of his efforts. I, however, am of the opinion that the change of nomenclature from 'Progressive' to 'Fragrant', from 'Progoti Sahitya Kanon' to 'Surabhi Sahitya Kanon' brought in its wake the fragrance of success.

Geographer, Silencer, Poet—what kind of names are these, then? Don't we have names of our own? Indeed we do, each one of us surely has a given name. But those names have no point to them. Whereas these three names—Geographer, Silencer, Poet—they have such a magnificent ring to them, do they not? What significant echoes are to be heard here, between very dissimilar consonances! Are you not curious, don't you want to know the origin of these names? How, may I ask, can I have brought you to this point in the story without arousing your curiosity? In that case, let me tell you the secret of this not-so-mysterious mystery.

The three of us are pundits. Learned men. No, by that I don't mean that we are extremely learned, but pundits in the sense that we are teachers. We teach in the same school. The three of us are from three different places. We have now settled down in the neighbourhood of the school. We are each other's devotees—not in matters of religion, but in all other ways. Geographer had come here as a teacher of Geography. Perhaps because he himself was not as rotund as the globe, he hated the subject of Geography the most.

It was a Venture School. That is, it had been established by the local people of the area, and had not yet received recognition from the authorities. For the best of reasons, the subject itself, Geography, was taken away from the curriculum in order to lighten the burden of academics on the students. Therefore Geographer took upon himself the responsibility of educating the students in the subject of literature. If the flame of his enthusiasm for literature had not been lit in this manner, this diligent endeavour of our lives—in other words, the aim of becoming life members of the Asomiya Sahitya Sanmilan—would have remained unfulfilled. Indeed, when I think of it now, my whole body trembles. (I hear somebody saying offstage that the sentence is bathetic. To him I reply, listen, we are not asking you for your pathetic opinion.)

Geographer's name had been given to him by the peon of our school, Bhobeen. (Not Bhoben or Bhobendra, for he gets annoyed if addressed as such). Bhobeen, of course, had respectfully addressed him as Geographer

Saar. Now we can hardly address our colleague as 'Saar', Sir. Therefore 'Saar' was lopped off. Even in the hustle and bustle of ringing the school bell, cheeky Bhobeen finds time to prepare some chewing tobacco for Geographer, because Geographer cannot prepare his own tobacco while taking a class. After he goes to take a class, Bhobeen calls out, 'Geographer Saar, Geographer Saar,' and passes on the tobacco to him on the sly. Everybody notices it, though Geographer assumes that nobody has, and passes the tobacco into his mouth, making a marble pop out on one side of his cheek.

The sad thing is that this scene cannot be witnessed these days. Since some time now, Geographer has promoted himself, and instead of chewing tobacco, has taken to puffing on cigarettes. Nobody knows the reason for this change. But I suspect that this calamity has occurred after 'Surabhi Sahitya Kanon' was accorded recognition by the Asomiya Sahitya Sanmilan. Calamity, because the geography of Geographer's face changes while he puffs on a cigarette. There is a dreadful focus, a terrible attentiveness in his face at that point, (Terrible attentiveness! Can attentiveness be terrible? Heh, who says it can't?) because when I see this, there is a kind of involuntary movement in my facial muscles, which can be called laughter, but we cannot laugh or smile. This is because Silencer and I have sworn to be eternal disciples of Geographer. For this reason, when Geographer puffs on his cigarette, my efforts to quell my laughter create a painful change in the geography of my facial muscles.

You've guessed quite right. Silencer's name, too, is the invention of Bhobeen's fertile mind. As inventions go, this one is excellent. If the question were to be asked: 'How to describe (Silencer's given name) in one word,' then it has to be said, 'That one word is Silencer'. His unique characteristic, his dharma, is that of quietude, or silence. It is not as though he does not have another characteristic, but because that is secondary, and subordinate to 'Silencer', it is unimportant. When Silencer becomes anybody's devotee or disciple, he keeps nodding his head at all the utterances of that person. At present he is Geographer's disciple. Everything that Geographer says meets with his silent approval, signified by his nods.

Since in Bhobeen's dictionary, Silence and Silencer are synonymous, the name of this friend of ours is Silencer. In any case the word Silencer is more sonorous than Silence, and has a nice ring to it.

Poet. That's me. It has not been necessary for Bhobeen to gift me with this name. I consider myself a poet. The name is the rightful recognition of my acknowledged work as a legitimate poet. And when even Geographer began to address me as Poet, I could not help but be drenched in the poetic creativity conveyed by the word. It is irrelevant to me whether and how any merchant of literature measures me on his scales of poetic achievement. It is enough that I have received this gratifying recognition from Geographer.

It is generally acknowledged among merchants of literature that there are two aspects to literature, literary criticism and so on. To put it in legal language, these two aspects are cognizable and non-cognizable.

The person who is most to be revered, whose lotus feet need to be worshipped the most, is the cognizable person, from whom one can get the most benefits. Category wise, the other cognizables are sometimes one's near ones, sometimes one's dear ones, sometimes people whom we think we should cultivate. Non-cognizables are to be ignored.

However, Geographer is not a merchant of literature. He is a biased connoisseur. That is why the recognition that he accords me is important to me. He has taken cognizance of my poems. Geographer offers critical comments on my poetic work. Oh yes, I ought to mention here what I teach at the school. Actually, I had not come to the school as a teacher at all. I had joined as a clerk. Some time later, when the Physical Training instructor of the school went away, I took his place. I think perhaps the cadences and rhythms of poetic thought began to knock around inside me as I tried to bring together the beats of the rhythmic drill during my Physical Training classes. How else could I have acquired poetic power as soon as I became a Physical Training instructor? Bhobeen is not aware that a poet is enshrined in his school. He has named me 'Diril Saar', his version of 'Drill Sir'. The word 'Diril' is perhaps poetic, but sometimes, when Bhobeen pronounces it in his crude tongue, 'Diril' sounds like 'Giril'. Giril, or Tumbled Down. It is for this reason that I do not like the name he has bestowed on me. I wish to be known as a creator of poesy, and prefer the name given to me by Geographer: Poet.

So much for the glory of our names. I am afraid that those who looked for a whiff of mystery, or had assumed that the names have some special, secret significance, will be disappointed. But it will not do if I do not tell you something of my poetic work. Geographer's role as friend, philosopher and guide will also become very clear in this. Silencer, of course, is silent. His opinions are carbon copies of Geographer's. He will therefore remain non-cognizable. When I showed Geographer my first poem he praised me quite a bit, saying, 'Hey, Poet, you've written quite a romantic poem!' I had heard the word romantic before, but I had not known what kind of poem was called romantic. Hearing Geographer's words, I understood that what I had written after seeing something that had thrilled and touched me, was in fact a romantic poem. I have already mentioned that I began my career as a poet when I became a Physical Training instructor. But on reflection, I think now that perhaps there may have been another reason also for the rousing of the yogic power, the kundalini of my poetic prowess. During that time, a young girl had come to work in our school for about three months on a leave vacancy. Whenever she was present in the teacher's common room, the young male teachers surrounded the place like flies gathering around molasses. This humble Poet (not yet a poet at that time) was no exception. I don't know exactly how it happened, but one day, while I was gazing at her petal-soft face, perhaps the gurgling stream in my breast suddenly woke up from a trance. A poet was born that very night. I wish to present a glimpse of those verses:

Your lotus face, as soft as butter,
Sets my heartbeats all a-flutter.

As soon as Geographer heard the poem, he declared, 'You've written a beautiful poem, Poet.'

Even though my inspiration, my muse, left us within three months, there was no way anybody could have stopped the poet within me from storming out. Just as the Ganga comes bursting out tumultuously from Gangotri on its journey to the Bay of Bengal, the swift currents of my poetry created turbulent waves as they rushed to fall into the ocean of Asomiya literature. This was the beginning.

'Prabahon',* the legendary Asomiya journal, was still being published at that time. When my poem appeared in it, I was so puffed up with pride that I could hardly come back to my senses. The magazine had been quite popular.

But 'Prabahon' breathed its last, and shuffled off its mortal coils. For a while, I was at a loss about what to do next. Then I realized that in the meantime, a new journal 'Kamdhenu'* was being published. I sent my poems there. They were returned. I sent them again. They were neither returned, nor acknowledged. Nor were they published. It was very disheartening. Poet was fast sinking.

---

*Prabahan, Kamdhenu: references to the well-known and trend-setting literary journals *Awahon* and *Ramdhenu* of several decades ago.

At this crucial moment, Geographer brought the life-giving herb sanjivani to Poet's dying heart. One day, Geographer asked, 'Listen, Poet, how come I haven't heard your poems for a long time?' I replied, 'It's not my writing that has stopped: there's been no let up there. It's the journal that has vanished. Listen to this…' In any case, I always carried my poems around in my pocket. I whipped out one of them, and began to read it out.

Geographer held up his hands and stopped me. His words were startling. 'Poet, my friend, the days of talking in this manner of the moon, the stars, cool zephyrs, life, boatmen, the rays of the sun, beloved—those days have gone, you know. Don't you realize that this is the age of Modern Poetry? Much water has flown down the bridge while you were up there floating around in the clouds, riding the balloon of your imagination.'

Ever since Geographer has become a literary sage, or a teacher, he has kept track of the latest books and trends. He is absolutely up-to-date about such matters. When Geographer talked in this way, I realized that there was some flaw somewhere in my work. I wondered to myself, 'Have the days of writing poems about the moon, about sweethearts gone, then? But the moon, the moonlight, and the beloved's moonlike face are still around.'

Perhaps Geographer was looking at my face. Seeming to sense my confusion, he said, 'In the part of the poem that you have just read out to me, the moon sends out its rays from behind the clouds, and your beloved's smile peeps out from behind her veil in the same way. Well, "peeps" is perhaps all right. But Poet, if one's feet are firmly on the ground, this same moon can be viewed in a different way, can it not? For instance, a hungry man will view the stained moon as a scorched roti. In this way, poets who write modern poetry have something new to say even about the moon, see? Your poetry will be modern only when it expresses what is truly modern in life. Life has become very complex, you know, Poet. (Did Geographer sigh? No, it was I who did.) The thoughts that come from this complex modern life to the modern poet are complex, too, and are expressed with complexity. You've eaten walnuts, haven't you? Its shell is hard, but once you break it open, its kernel is tasty. Modern poetry is like that. You get to the kernel only after you break open the shell of the walnut. The kernel is dry, but it has taste and flavour. You write poetry when inspiration strikes you, making your heart molten in the process, and you pour it out like you pour out water. But modern poets don't write like that, see?'

Geographer gave me lots of tips after this. Even better, he gave me a book of modern poetry. With Geographer's advice, and after reading that book, it did not take long for me to metamorphose into a modern poet. However, 'Kamdhenu' kept rejecting my poems. But so what? I met up with several colleagues and other like-minded people who had been rejected by 'Kamdhenu'. With money from our own pockets, we brought out a mini magazine. Geographer was of course with us as advisor, and to 'bolster' Geographer's 'opinion' (since I have doubts about how these two words, 'bolster' and 'opinion' are pronounced, it's better to write them in the Roman script) Silencer, too, joined our group. Every nod of his head seemed to convey the hidden praises of a hundred connoisseurs. Geographer even went to the extent of writing a laudatory piece of criticism under an assumed name. And in the end, the 'Progoti Sahitya Kanon' was born. Since the progress of the 'Progoti Sahitya Kanon' was obstructed, 'Progoti' or progress itself was abandoned. Now we spread the fragrance of modern poetry through the 'Surabhi Sahitya Kanon.'

And today, Geographer, Silencer and I, that is, Poet, have arrived at the railway station to attend the annual conference of the greatly respected literary organization, the Asomiya Sahitya Sanmelan as the accredited representatives of its recognized chapter.

Geographer and Silencer have set out for the Sanmelan with high enthusiasm. I should have been doubly enthused, for I am a poet. My poetry would be uproariously welcomed by the enthusiastic applause of thousands of connoisseurs at the conference. Yet even though I was pleased and excited, that excitement was a little subdued. In the thrill of realizing that I would be taking part in the conference as a member, I had bravely dashed off forty poems. I had then entrusted Geographer with the task of selecting ten poems out of those forty. Just yesterday, Geographer had given me those ten poems. But he had in addition, unloosed an opinion 'Look here, Poet. You still seem to be wandering through the mansions of modern poetry. But try to climb down from those mansions. Turning up your nose at the world, and penning modern poetry won't do, won't do at all. Wrinkling your nose in disgust you are still sitting in that mansion, trying to gather up the shattered pieces and searching for patterns in them. It was okay when you did that earlier, when it was acceptable. But you will have to become post-modern now.'

I am startled at this opinion of Geographer's. In addition there is Silencer's nodding head. I have brought along to the Sahitya Sanmelan the poems that Geographer had chosen, but his opinion of the previous day keeps rankling. Geographer is a person who is abreast of all the latest literary trends. Coming as they do from a senior, his opinions have significance and importance. But is it possible to become a post-modern just because somebody tells you to? Unless Geographer explains it all to me, how will I know what this post-modern poetry is? He was so rushed yesterday, he had no time to do so. The geography of his face had assumed an unnaturally serious expression, and he had downed shutters on the post office of post-modernism.

Therefore, even though I carry the burden of my poems in my pocket, I am a worried person when I reach the railway station. As soon as we set foot on platform number seven, an announcement over the tannoy tells us that our train is two hours late. Geographer furrows his brow. At the same time, Silencer, too, changes the geography of his facial contours, and sends waves running along the line of his brows. Since thoughts of post-modernism are creating a turmoil in my mind, the announcement provokes no reaction in me. Pointing to a concrete bench at the eastern end of the platform, Geographer says, 'Come, let us rest there.' Suitcases by our side, the three of us sit on the bench. As soon as he sits down, Geographer says, 'Annoying.'

Here is my opportunity. I know from experience that whenever Geographer is annoyed, his annoyance evaporates like camphor, and his heart fills with profound truths, if he can get hold of a subject dear to his heart on which he can hold forth. Sometimes, to flatter him, I address Geographer as Kokaiti, or Elder Brother. Now I ask him, 'Kokaiti, you had told me yesterday to write post-modern poetry. Since then, I have been thinking about it. I realize now that I will have to become a post-modern poet. I shall never forget how you inspired me long ago to write modern poetry. To tell you the truth, I've been going ahead on the strength of what you told me then. Just teach me this post-modernism, and I will be able to pass the rest of my days safely…'

I notice the spot in the middle of Geographer's forehead, where his eyebrows meet, become darker. I realize that bright rays of wisdom will now pop out, grasshopper-fashion. (Thoughts that pop out grasshopper-fashion leap out like those insects. I have to admit, however, that I sometimes have to try quite desperately to find the coupling between diverse images.)

In a grave and serious voice, Geographer says, 'Ah,

Poet, you are in a post-modern situation, yet you don't see post-modernism. Do you see this railway station? This is nothing but post-modernism.'

This weighty pronouncement startles me somewhat. I have been thinking of the railway station in terms of modernism, as a realistic example of the progress from animal-drawn carts to the civilization of machines. However, I am totally out of my depth when confronted with the noise and confusion of a railway station. A long time ago, searching for order within this confusion, I had even penned a poem. I had discovered the connection in this manner: the station captures some moments in the lives of the people as they journey through life. At that time, Geographer had praised me mightily after reading the verses in which I had made the station a symbol of one such moment. And now here is Geographer, insisting that the station is actually post-modern.

I am confused. These days, Geographer reads a lot of English and Bangla books. Since he finds it a little difficult to go through books written in English, he reads mostly Bangla books, and from these, he extracts a variety of thoughts, which seem to sprout antennae in all directions. With those antennae, Geographer snags nourishing vitamins from the local air, and after grinding them in the mills of his mind, finally gives us a capsule of his original theories. After swallowing his capsule on modernism, I have remained a modernist. Now, since it appears that Geographer is getting ready to deliver a capsule on post-modernism, I get ready to swallow it preparatory to suffering from indigestion.

Geographer begins. 'This station that you see is a collection of a vast variety of objects. At this place is the foul odour of left-over food that has been dumped as garbage; there, on the platform's TV screen is the highbrow classical dance of a Mumbai heroine. Soldiers. Veiled Marwari ladies. There on that bench, a pair of lovers. Railway workers moving about unconcernedly. Policemen. Travellers, speaking in many different tongues. Everybody is carrying around their own individual worlds with them. Yet they are all present in this very station, that is, they are present at the same time, in the same place. This is the present. You, as a poet, see all this as fragments, as confusion and, grimacing in disdain, take refuge in your own mansion of modernity. Within that mansion, you join these fragmentary scenes together to create an image. You are desperate to find some deeper meaning, a hidden significance, in all this. But if you were a post-modernist, you would have seen that the present is after all like this—each object with its own individual character, busy in its own field of action. Individuals may come together at a railway station, at the same time, in the same place. If the station master of this railway station decides to clean up and get rid of all the confusion and uproar in this place by forcing everybody onto the same train and sending them off in the same direction, then obviously there will be chaos. Modern poets such as you view the station as disorderly, but see the station master's train as orderly. In your eyes, whatever is orderly is beautiful. This uproar is ugly because it is chaotic.

Sending everybody off on the same train is orderly, therefore it is beautiful. You yourself wish to have nothing to do with this disorder. On the other hand, you want to impose order on the confusion and uproar. And since you cannot achieve this order through action, you try to do so through poetry. You search out the hidden significance and deeper meanings, and try to view them through the lenses of imposed orderliness and remain self-absorbed within your own mansion of modernity, immersed in images you have created.'

I don't understand a thing. Have I done some wrong in trying to be a modernist? Will everything become all right if I can become a post-modernist, then? Long ago, Geographer had given me his own theory of modernism. Now he wants to give me his own views on the theory of post-modernism. At that time, I had been able to become a modern poet, but now everything seems to have become a tangled mess.

But Geographer has not yet come to the end of his theory. Imbuing his facial expression with yet more gravity, he begins his speech once more, 'Look here, Poet, the days of the Grand Narrative are now over.'

Grand Narrative? What Grand Narrative is this Geographer talking about? Either my brain is haemorrhaging, or the Grand Narrative has morphed into a graceful dancing boy. Everything has turned topsy-turvy; I feel as though a kind of post-modern chaos is churning within me.

It seems that post-modern Geographer has got some

inkling of what I am thinking. Bringing an expression of understanding to his face, he says, 'For example, look at you. You have taken the scenes piece-meal, and are trying to put them together in your mind in an orderly manner. Suppose you are about to string together a garland of flowers. (Hadn't he talked earlier of creating a picture?) You will have to thread a needle before you begin. The needle is needed in order to string the flowers into a garland. So too, in this case. Modern man creates theories in his search for the meaning of life. (Isn't this what he, too, is doing?) Suppose that to be the needle. A Grand Narrative is created in this search for the meaning of life. With great difficulty, a single interpretation, a sole explanation to fit every aspect of life is created. A single string is found running through each and every thing. But, Poet, if you look carefully, you will see that there are several strings that run in many directions. The garlands have been strung on different needles. If, in your attempt to combine everything together into one garland, you find that the flowers on one of the strands are not going well with the rest, you throw away that strand. Another strand clashes with the rest. You discard that, as well. But even though those strands have been discarded, they still exist. It is just that you, Poet, pretend not to see them, for they do not exist within your Grand Narrative. This kind of thing just won't do, don't you see? It is the sheer use of force. Grand Narratives use force, whereas post-modernism does not believe in the use of force of this kind.'

A whirlwind seems to have entered my mind. I don't know which theorist's ideas Geographer has purloined to invent this String Theory, but I feel that he has unleashed a local version of this theory. Well, so be it. Fake interpretations suit us best. I dare to ask him, 'In that case, is it best to go in for Little Narratives in post-modernism?'

Geographer is staring at me with a somewhat belittling look. He replies, 'Don't call it Little Narrative. Call it Local Narrative, instead. And, Poet, why on earth do you use the words "it is best to go in for"? Don't say such a thing. Admit that it is already in existence, is extant.'

I realize now that Geographer is a merchant of post-modern ideas. I begin to suspect him of trying to sell the fruits of his subject, Geography, as the fruits of literature. Luckily, this suspicion of mine is not visible on my face. If it had, Geographer would no doubt have spurned this modern doubt of mine as being of a suspicious nature. But his pronouncements are not over yet. For, with a focussed, almost reverential concentration, he begins to regurgitate his theories once more. (This modern/post-modern dichotomy seems to me as confusing as the one god/many god theory.) 'Local Narratives denote the multitude of spheres to be found in life, such as the spheres of work, religion, literature, culture, politics. In other words, as people move around within their own spheres of work, they create a language for their own individual and specialized needs. No doubt, in the swift pace of life, the distance between these various spheres has diminished greatly. They jostle each other, rub shoulders with each other, fall on top of each other. But none of them can erase any of the others by violent means. It is the violence of the Grand Narrative that tries to do so. Therefore, let all Local Narratives continue.

What else is it but peaceful co-existence? You will see that peace will reign.'

In the Chaotic Narrative of the station, Geographer's speech seems like a Grand Narrative to me. My head is beginning to ache. I see a man approach. He is selling spiced gram. This spicy snack always clears my head of doubts and confusion. I therefore call out to him, and buy a rupee's worth of spiced gram from him.

Geographer's expounding has dimmed everything into a thick haze. It seems he is still not satisfied, however, for he asks the gram-seller, 'Listen, do you keep cigarettes? Give me a stick.'

Cigarettes and spiced gram can only co-exist in post-modernism. The gram seller, however, is a traditional person. He says, 'Sir, I don't keep cigarettes, but they are available in that stall over there. Shall I bring you some?'

'All right then, bring me a packet,' says Geographer. He gives him money for a pack of cigarettes. I, too, hand over some money and ask him to bring me another packet. Munching on the spiced gram, I look around to see the various kinds of Local Narratives around me. I can see one field of Local Narrative represented by the three of us, that is, the field of literature. Those armymen who are sitting on their bed rolls and eating food from their tiffin carriers, do they symbolize the field of war, then? Goodness, there is such a variety of fields to be found amidst the yawning, bored-looking travellers here. That spiced-gram vendor who has gone to a stall to get some cigarettes for Geographer and me, I suppose he, too, has his own field and narrative.

Just as I am perusing this line of thought, an earth-shaking explosion rents the air. There are screams and shouts all around, chaos everywhere. Piteous wails of agony can be heard. At the same time, the lights go off. The platform is plunged into darkness.

A powerful bomb explosion has taken place in the middle of the platform where we sit, waiting. The thought comes to my mind that a Narrative has exploded here: the post-modern narrative of somebody who does not believe in Grand Narratives. All other narratives have been obliterated in chaos and confusion.

Running helter-skelter, Geographer stands up, and grabs his suitcase. (Ask the expert in figures of speech whether one can run helter-skelter and stand up at the same time or not.) Silencer imitates Geographer. I stand up as well, but keep staring dazedly at the place where the bomb has exploded, for I had noticed that the spiced-gram vendor whom we had sent off for cigarettes had just reached the stall where the bomb had exploded. Could he still possibly be alive?

Geographer grabs me by the hand, and tugs at me. The geography of his face has changed. A harassed look has come upon it. He says, 'Come, Poet, come on! It's best to go from here as soon as possible. The police and the Army will come and cordon off this place completely. They will question everybody. We cannot get involved in all these complications.'

'Many people must have died,' I say. 'We ought to go and help. At least that gram vendor…'

Geographer interrupts me scornfully. Saying 'Thuri… Hang your gram vendor,' he grabs me by the hand and pulls me out of the station. The three of us return home in two autos.

The newspaper arrives first at Geographer's house. I therefore go early in the morning to his house to have a look at the paper. Silencer has already arrived there. As soon as the paper is delivered, all three of us fall eagerly upon it. It is Geographer who first raises his head. The geography of his face is calm and peaceful, his voice is detached. He announces, 'Thank God, nobody we know has died.' (From the list of names of the dead and their professions that has appeared in the paper, I have surmised that the spiced-gram vendor is not among the mortally wounded.)

The significance of this utterance of Geographer's—that nobody we know has died—is that the news item that says that seven people have been killed is actually quite insignificant. It is as though the number seven is just that: a number, with no reference to human lives at all. From Silencer's vigorously nodding head it can be surmised that this utterance is true. However, I am absolutely panic-stricken. Geographer looks at me in surprise. He asks, 'What's the matter with you then, Poet? Your face looks quite anaemic.'

I am unable to say anything. Instead, I point to a portion of the news item, which reveals that an unclaimed suitcase has been found at the site. The initials of a person's name are written on this piece of luggage. The authorities have not yet revealed those initials because their investigations are still underway. But it is suspected that the suitcase belongs to a miscreant.

The same words come out simultaneously from the mouths of both Geographer and Silencer: 'Did you leave your suitcase behind?' Usually, Silencer only nods. But now, after a long time, he has sung a duet with Geographer. The comically imitative grace of Silencer's voice splashes over my forlorn face, and aggravates my agony and misery even further.

I can already hear the march of policemen's booted feet. In my imagination, the strokes of their hands become a post-modern truth. And on my back, they distribute the sound of slashes.

A Mote in the Eye

Holding his father's hand, a young boy went for an outing to the highest hill in the city. At the topmost point of that hill was a very tall wireless reception tower. From its base to its top, the tower became progressively thinner. Its base was at an angle of precisely ninety degrees, exactly as though it was created by two straight lines. It was possible to circumambulate the base of this lofty tower and view the city spread out below, and it was for this reason that the father had brought his son here.

They were not alone. A man had put up a telescope at the base of the tower, and was completely engrossed in studying some distant point in the skies. Even though the boy's father had never spoken to the person, he recognized him. He did not wish to disturb the man who was so intent in his observations. However, he did feel some curiosity about why the man kept staring fixedly at the boundless sky day after day in this manner.

He walked around cautiously today, holding the boy's hand so that the man's concentration was not disturbed. But the boy, looking with great curiosity at the man, asked his father in a piercing voice, 'Deuta, what is that man looking at like that?' He had spoken so loudly that it was impossible for the man not to hear his words. The father felt a little uneasy, and putting his forefinger to his mouth, he signalled, 'Quiet!'

This time, the little boy murmured, 'What is the man doing, Deuta?' Even though the boy had asked the question in a whisper, in this lonely place, it sounded quite loud. Confused, the father whispered back, very softly, 'He is conducting research.' (He did not know if he was actually doing any research or not, but he could find no better answer to give to the child.) The boy was not yet of an age to understand what the word 'research' meant. Therefore, to understand the meaning of 'research', he kept looking around curiously to study the man even as he went about with his father.

The man noticed nothing of this. He was totally engrossed in his study. The boy's father decided that it was better to hurry away from that place before the boy again made him uncomfortable with more awkward questions. He went back to the car that was parked some distance away, and left.

This scene was not an unusual one. It was natural for the boy to be curious. It was also normal for his father to assume that the man was engaged in some kind of research. This person, standing beside the city's tallest tower, rising up in a pure straight line, patiently focussed his telescope at a distant point in the universe. He was looking for an original discovery. If we were to look away from his fixed gaze, and draw an imaginary line to that distant point, we would assume that that would be a straight line of extraordinary length.

But our story does not end here. The origin of every extraordinary invention is an ordinary event. Take Newton, for example. If that apple hadn't plunged down…! Or Archimedes. Yes indeed, Archimedes. But before that, I wish to talk about a few small events that are connected to a minor incident.

Shrimati Bordoloi was worried. People do get worried, but her fretfulness was about her husband. Her prime concern about her spouse was that Mr Bordoloi was a social activist who had taken upon himself to whip up social consciousness, and this made her constantly anxious.

A society cannot develop along a straight pathway. There are bound to be bends on the road. That, at least, was Shrimati Bordoloi's notion. She believed that if one could mould oneself to these bends, adapt to them, and proceed accordingly, things would jog along quite smoothly. Everything would then appear to be straight. Bordoloi did not think in this manner, and he became quite noisy when he discussed this with eloquence. His voice was loud and penetrating, his writings powerful. People praised him if they had no vested interest. If his words clashed with a personal belief of theirs, or with their own vested interests, they would criticize him while out of earshot, without actually mentioning his name. If Bordoloi's or Shrimati Bordoloi's relations and acquaintances got to hear these, they felt uncomfortable. Lacking the courage to relay this to Bordoloi himself, they would catch Shrimati Bordoloi's ear: 'You should tell him, there's no point messing about in things that don't concern him.'

'Is it really necessary to do all this? People badmouth him and call him a wild dog.'

And so on.

Because of his strongly developed sense of social consciousness, Bordoloi did not care a bit for what people might say. Besides, he had a very strong sense of self-pride. It was because of this same pride that he did not go for a doctorate degree even after intensely researching a complex subject. Bordoloi did not think that a doctoral degree was suitable for himself after Dutta, his contemporary, a lecturer and colleague in the same college, received his doctoral degree by copying others' notes and polishing them up. It was because of the boundless confidence that he had in his own learning that he began to ignore doctoral degree holders and belittle them. However, he deeply desired recognition in his workplace. Even though his ego would not allow him to say so openly, he coveted the post of Principal of his college. But when the time came, he was denied this post. Dr Dutta, expert in his field of study, became the Principal. Ever since then, Bordoloi began to disparage those who held official designations.

Bordoloi was an 'original thinker'. Actually, this amounted to him presenting a totally dissimilar opinion and a very different point of view about a subject from those other thinkers who had studied it and discoursed on it. Bordoloi thought this to be a sign of his unique mode of thinking. But others saw it as convoluted, and also slandered it.

Shrimati Bordoloi was always worried about her husband getting embroiled in a variety of arguments. These anxieties increased when a colleague of Bordoloi's came with a complaint against him to Shrimati Bordoloi. This complainant was none other than Dr Dutta, who was not simply Bordoloi's colleague, but also the new Principal of his college. Whatever Bordoloi's opinion about Dutta's intelligence, because of his post he was now senior to Bordoloi in the organizational hierarchy. The reins of the college, too, were in his hands now. This same Dutta told Shrimati Bordoloi that Bordoloi had taken to ridiculing him. According to Dutta, it was only because of their friendship and the demands of civility that he had not let word of the happenings spread further.

Even after discounting all possible exaggerations, when Shrimati Bordoloi thought about it, she realized that there was every possibility of major problems arising if the matter was not taken in hand. According to Dr Dutta, he was building a beautiful ceremonial gateway to commemorate the golden jubilee of the college. He was supervising this glorious task himself, so that it could be executed to perfection. But Bordoloi had suddenly rushed into the Principal's office the other day without rhyme or reason and said that the ceremonial gateway was all bent. Why had not a responsible person like Principal Dutta noticed that the gateway was so very crooked? (Dr Dutta had felt that Bordoloi had pronounced the word 'responsible' in a warped and twisted kind of way.) Who would be answerable for this enormous wastage?

Dr Dutta had been away in Delhi for about fifteen days on work with the UGC. He therefore thought that some big mess-up had occurred while he had been away. He went immediately to the gate and examined it thoroughly. He was quite astonished at what he saw.

Not because the gate was crooked, but because it stood up straight and proud. There was no foundation for Bordoloi's accusation. In other words, Bordoloi had ridiculed him. Dr Dutta told Shrimati Bordoloi that if any other colleague had said something like this, he would have taken stern steps. But Bordoloi was not just his colleague, he was also his contemporary. Besides, he was his friend, and also somebody whose learning he admired. (Dr Dutta did not mention that his strange theories were comical.) It was for these reasons that he had come to let Shrimati Bordoloi know of these matters. (In other words, Shrimati Bordoloi could not rein in her husband, who had crossed all bounds of decency and was creating problems. He became quite excited while saying this.)

Shrimati Bordoloi had yet another cause for worry. They had been invited to a community dinner that had been organized on the occasion of the festivities connected with the Golden Jubilee functions of the college, and Shrimati Bordoloi had gone there with her husband. She noticed that her husband's face had become pinched with dissatisfaction at the glittering event. Even though she sat and chatted with the other invited women, she kept an eye on Bordoloi from a distance. She was concerned that her husband would profess some opinion that would not be in tune with the situation, and make her, along with others, quite distraught. She saw Bordoloi go up to Dr Dutta and, pointing towards his tie, say something. Dr Dutta became suspicious. Glancing at Bordoloi's face, he went quickly towards the washroom. On his return, he looked with exasperation at Bordoloi. Moving away, Dr Dutta tried to avoid him thereafter.

Shrimati Bordoloi, who had been keeping a close watch on her husband, realized that he had said something to annoy Dr Dutta. She went towards Bordoloi. On seeing her, Bordoloi said in quite a loud voice, 'You know, this Dutta likes to wear ties, but doesn't know how to knot it properly. Did you notice how he has worn it, so crookedly? I pointed it out to him, but he has continued to wear it as crookedly as ever.'

Bordoloi said all this quite stridently. Thankfully, there were no people nearby, and an embarrassing situation was prevented. Shrimati Bordoloi thought, maybe it was true, Dr Dutta had perhaps knotted his tie in a hurry, making it hang crookedly. Even so, it was hardly necessary for her husband to point this out to Dr Dutta. At the very moment that this thought came to her mind, Dr Dutta came forward and informed Shrimati Bordoloi that dinner had been served. With some irritation, he glanced at Bordoloi, who was looking the other way. It was then that Shrimati Bordoloi noticed Dr Dutta's tie. Why, it was quite neat, falling from his neck with precision. In the meantime, Bordoloi was advancing towards the dining table. Taking this opportunity, Dr Dutta told Shrimati Bordoloi quite gravely, 'Perhaps you should get his eyes checked? Sometimes, if both eyes are not working in synchronization, it can lead to things being perceived to be crooked.'

Shrimati Bordoloi became quite anxious. She grew very worried. For the actual significance of what Dr Dutta was trying to tell her was that his tie was perfectly straight, and it was Bordoloi's eyesight that was at fault. As Bordoloi's wife, it was her duty to get his eyes examined by an optician.

Shrimati Bordoloi knew the terrible uproar that would follow if she advised her husband to visit the optician. The kind of faith that Bordoloi, with his firm belief in himself, had in both his inner and outer vision made it impossible to raise questions before him in a straightforward manner.

Shrimati Bordoloi could not place before her husband any proposal to visit the optician. The incident was beginning to fade from her memory. But a third thing happened, and this had nothing to do with Dr Dutta.

For some time, Bordoloi had been writing furiously about the inefficiency of the State Electricity Board. He was uncaring about whether his writings actually affected anybody or not. But one day Bordoloi lost all patience. On a very muggy summer day, the Electricity Board cut the supply of electricity to their entire neighbourhood for the whole day. Bordoloi's study was a sunless room. It was not possible to read there even during the daytime unless there was electricity. Sweating profusely in that terrible heat, unable to read, he became quite irritated.

When Bordoloi made enquiries about the matter, he found out that the Board was erecting new pillars to improve the electrical supply. It was for that reason that the electric supply was cut temporarily. Bordoloi, being a very socially aware person, immediately set out to inspect the way the pillars were being installed. He believed that it was necessary for the public to be vigilant in order to prevent any slackness by the useless department. But he returned quickly. The sound of the gate clanging shut was by itself enough to make Shrimati Bordoloi realize that he had come back in a towering rage. As soon as he returned, he stood in front of Shrimati Bordoloi as usual and began to roundly rebuke the Electricity Board.

'Look here, just look at what they are up to! They've set up the posts all crooked! When I pointed it out, they said that they've set them up quite straight. What nonsense! That neighbour of ours, Dhiresh Babu, was passing by. I called him over and showed him the posts. He just muttered something and went off. You know our people don't have any civic awareness. They do whatever they like. People don't raise their voices at all!'

After a while, his roars and fulminations stopped. He

had a lot of work to do. He could not spend too much time on a single matter. But when Shrimati Bordoloi went as usual for her evening walk with her husband, she saw, to her amazement that the electric posts that had been newly installed by the Electricity Board were standing erect, at a ninety-degree angle to the ground. Seeing the posts, Bordoloi paused, and began to give vent to his anger very loudly. 'Look, look, do you see these posts? Do you see how crooked they are? These people, they're such shirkers when it comes to work…'

In spite of what he said, Shrimati Bordoloi could find no bent post. Even though she was confused, she remained silent and became quite anxious. She was now convinced that something had gone seriously wrong with her husband's eyesight. Several other such incidents increased her anxiety. She was also surprised to notice that Bordoloi did not perceive all things to be bent or twisted. He perceived specific objects to be bent at particular times, at which point his social consciousness would also raise its head vigorously. Shrimati Bordoloi did not object in any way to this awakening of social consciousness. But she feared that if this problem continued, her conscientious husband might become the butt of insults.

So far, Bordoloi's problems with his vision had occurred outside the house, in the public domain. Shrimati Bordoloi thought that it was there that Bordoloi was forced to become socially alert and active. But on the day that this problem with his vision came into the domestic sphere, Shrimati Bordoloi grew alarmed.

She was having a new room built in the house without Bordoloi's consent. Their only child had always been out of town, studying away from home. Now that he had grown up, he was returning home. A special room was urgently required for him, but Bordoloi thought that to be a waste. He was a boy who had grown up outside, studying in schools away from his hometown. He would be living away from this place. When he came home occasionally, it would be as a guest only. Why the need for a special room for him now? However, this difference of opinion had not created any rift between the two of them. Bordoloi had not actually stopped her from building the room either.

One day, Shrimati Bordoloi was busy in the kitchen. The carpenter was fixing the door frame. After returning from college, Bordoloi had gone with a certain curiosity to watch the progress of the work on the room. Suddenly, from inside the kitchen itself, Shrimati Bordoloi heard her husband's loud rants. He was yelling at the carpenter. Hearing the word 'crooked' several times in the flow of abuse, she hurried to her roaring husband. She saw that he was pointing towards the door frame and shouting to the carpenter, 'Take it off! Take it off just now! You wicked carpenter, you've fixed it crookedly before my very eyes!'

The carpenter dangled his plumb line from the top of the frame, and said, 'No, huzoor. Look, the frame is absolutely straight.'

Bordoloi grew even more infuriated at the carpenter's

rebuttal. His yells grew even louder. Shrimati Bordoloi saw that the frame was absolutely perpendicular, and yet her husband was seeing it as crooked. She knew that this was not the time to raise her voice or protest. She therefore signalled the carpenter to go away. Calming down her husband, she brought him inside the house, assuring him that she would see to it that the matter was soon remedied.

Seeing stars, the astounded carpenter stopped coming from that day. The door frame remained as he had left it, and Shrimati Bordoloi now had to go out and look for another carpenter. It was not that she had any objections to searching for another workman. After all, she was the one who shouldered all domestic responsibilities, since her husband was so busy in the sphere of social alertness and activism. He had no time for these domestic difficulties. It was for another reason, therefore, that Shrimati Bordoloi was at her wits' end with worry. She was convinced that there was something wrong with her husband's eyes, and unless it was treated quickly, there would be some calamity. But how could she propose to her husband that he should visit the optician?

Bordoloi had a strong ego, and was also very self assured. This was why he never wavered from his principles. He was also proud of his sharp vision. He even believed that the acuity of his vision contributed to the straightforwardness of his ideas. But for some time now, Bordoloi's self assurance was being eroded. Though his ego did not allow him to acknowledge this fact, he was certainly seeing certain objects as crooked, and others did not agree with this perspective of his. (Even his wife did not agree with it. She had not voiced her opinion on it, but Bordoloi could make out what she thought). This had sown some seeds of doubt in his self assurance. But his ego was such that he began to assert his principles and point of view even more strongly, in order to cover up these seeds of doubt. To reinforce this, he began to say that even those objects that he did not perceive to be bent were in fact crooked.

When others looked at him suspiciously, he would insist even more strongly on this imaginary crookedness. By so doing, he would create a kind of reverse conviction in his own mind. In other words, he covered up the flaws of his own perception by insisting on the crookedness of something that was actually straight. But as soon as others expressed their disagreement, he began to actually believe that the object was really bent. However, in the very next moment, he would lose the firmness of his belief. It was just his ego, ultimately, that prevented him from saying that he wished to go to an optician to get his eyes examined.

Shrimati Bordoloi was not aware of this condition of his mind. But she hit on a plan to take her husband to the eye specialist. She told her husband that her own eyes were giving her a lot of trouble, and she wished to go to the optician to get them examined. She gathered up her courage and suggested that in addition, Bordoloi, too, could utilize this opportunity and get his own eyes examined. She added the logic: after all, age was catching up with them, it was prudent to get one's eyes examined now and again, etc., etc. Bordoloi was relieved to get this suggestion from his wife about a matter that his own ego prevented him from bringing up. To her surprise, he agreed to her proposal quite readily.

When the optician, after examining Bordoloi's eyes said that his eyesight was still sharp, and he had no need for glasses, Shrimati Bordoloi's worries, instead of decreasing, increased. If his eyesight was so good, why then did he perceive some objects to be bent? (These days, Bordoloi had started once more to insist that all vertical objects were bent. Not because he saw them as bent, but because he thought of them as crooked.) Was there some kind of fundamental error lodged in his mind then?

The surprising thing was that Bordoloi himself became worried. In his egoistic self-pride, he did not wish to acknowledge his mistake. On the other hand, his convictions were floundering. He therefore went in secret to see a psychiatrist. When the doctor said that he was free from any psychiatric problems, his worries, like those of his wife, grew even greater. He had in the meantime become certain that those whom he saw as crooked were perceived by others to be quite straight. If his eyesight was perfectly all right, if he had not fallen into the clutches of any mental disorders, then it meant that he was not in some kind of delirium. But what, then, could be the logical reason for this occurrence?

There were two effects of this. One of the effects was on his body. As soon as he saw a straight object, which he perceived to be crooked, he immediately bent his body to a synchronous angle, and began to walk in a slant exactly reflecting his perception. This came to him unconsciously. Bordoloi tried to align his body to become parallel to the bent object, in order to straighten the object itself. His manner of walking created curiosity. He was totally oblivious to this. (Even though Shrimati Bordoloi was anxious, there was nothing she could do about it. During their evening walks, she was the companion of her husband's bent posture. The curious glances of passers-by were aimed also at her.)

Secondly, because there was no apparent reason for this crookedness in his sight, an agitation was born in his mind. Bordoloi had always put forward his opinions through logic in the societal sphere. He began to believe that this twisted vision also had a theoretical logic in that sphere as well. He gradually became engrossed in theoretical research. As a result, without him being really conscious of it, Bordoloi began to move away from his self-appointed role of social activist and whip, and became quite immersed in philosophical research. He entered a pit, and, digging ever deeper, began to search for ancient roots to his theories. Others thought him to be crazy. Shrimati Bordoloi was bewildered. But Bordoloi was totally immersed in his enquiry.

In the beginning, we had mentioned that every extraordinary discovery has its beginning in ordinary events. Perhaps not everything can be generalized in this way, but we can certainly say that many important discoveries were made through a minor event. If an apple had not plummeted down, Newton would not have discovered the force of gravity. If a mishap had not occurred to the research on moulds, Alexander Fleming could not have discovered penicillin. Archimedes would not have been able to prove whether or not there were impurities in gold if he had not discovered a law while in the tub in the bathroom.

Bordoloi was thinking of such things while in his own bathroom. He thought of Newton and Archimedes. The impurities or 'crookedness' of gold—as soon as these words came to his mind, the word 'bent' suddenly popped up in his consciousness in connection with the word 'crookedness'. At that very moment, his gaze went through the gap in the skylight of the bathroom. He seemed to see a meteor fall in a crooked line towards the earth. Newton's law of gravity also came to his mind. In his consciousness glowed the conviction that in the entire universe, there was no such thing as a straight line. The gravity of all physical matters had bent everything. The concept of the straight line was an incorrect one. Like Archimedes, he became quite excited at his discovery, and ran out, practically naked, shouting 'Eureka! Eureka!'

(Civilization has evolved. He could not run completely naked through the streets like Archimedes had. Therefore, he somehow covered his nakedness with a gamosa.) Shrimati Bordoloi, who was busy in the kitchen, rushed out on hearing these shouts, and saw this half-crazed theoretician in an almost naked condition. She stared at him in astonishment.

Forgetting himself completely, Bordoloi announced his epochal theory to his wife, 'There is no such thing as a straight line, do you understand? There is no straight line! Everything in the universe is crooked, bent.' Shrimati Bordoloi could not comprehend that there was a philosophical discovery behind the ailment of the eyes that the optician could not find, the disorder which the psychiatrist could not discover. She thought that this was her husband's madness. Tears streamed down from her eyes.

But Bordoloi's mind was quite lost in contemplation. He was strong in his self belief. The world was being created through crookedness—this was the philosophical idea that his mind had now arrived at. The straight lines seen by ordinary people were a delusion, an optical illusion. He had been seeing crookedness in the middle of linearity. These were portents of the great discovery that he had been about to make. The straight signal of the all-pervasive crookedness of the universe!

Do you remember? A small boy had questioned his father with curiosity on seeing a man beside the perpendicular tower on the highest summit of the city, intently observing some distant point in the sky through his telescope. The man with the telescope was Bordoloi, the hero of our story. What exactly was he looking at so intently, at that distant point in the sky? Actually, every action has a reaction, and every concept has an anti-concept. It is the anti-concept that sheds clarity on the contours of the concept. After his discovery, Bordoloi was of the opinion that if every line in the universe was bent, there was sure to be a straight line in opposition to it, somewhere, which was concealed as the corresponding antithesis of the crooked line. This discovery would be the incontrovertible proof of his thesis. He was searching through his telescope in the distant skies for this ancient, single, unique straight line.

Shrimati Bordoloi did not understand these amazing theories. She was terrified of these unearthly actions of her husband's. She felt that the straight line of her life had been unalterably bent. There was nothing she could do except shed tears.

Love: An Essay

The subject of the very first essay that our teacher Bapi Bora Sir set for us was 'The Cow'. He also told us what the essay should contain. It was compulsory to put in the fact that the cow is a domestic animal. It was also necessary to catalogue the body parts of the cow, and give the number of legs, mouths, eyes, and tails that each possessed. The cow's colouring—whether it was brown, or dappled or anything else, had to be mentioned, and also what it ate—grass, grains, etc. The essay also had to contain information about the animal's nature, the work it did, the healthful qualities of cow's milk, the special quality of its hooves.

Bapi Sir placed a great deal of importance on the fact that cows chewed the cud. (When Bapi Sir chomped on betel nut, it looked as though he was chewing the cud). Each one of us wrote the composition, and showed it to Bapi Sir, and he remarked, 'Wonderful!' or 'Good,' etc., and marked the essays accordingly.

I ended my essay with the words, 'Cows are of great help to people. Therefore we should all love cows.' Bapi

Sir became quite rapturous at this. Exclaiming, 'Brilliant! Magnificent!' he gave me nine marks out of ten.

Bapi Sir made us write essays only on animals. He had no idea that there could be other topics besides these. Leaving aside the holidays, we had to turn out an essay a month, that is, about eight or nine of them a year. Bapi Sir did not have that many topics to set us. After essays on four or five different kinds of animals he would repeat the topics and make us write about those same animals all over again. The English word 'repeat' was a favourite of Sir's.

Next year, it was Dighol Sir who arrived on the scene, for we had been promoted. The various teachers did not get promoted along with the students. That was the rule. Otherwise, Bapi Sir would also have come up through the various grades along with us. Actually, Dighol Sir's name was not 'Dighol' at all. Indeed, we did not find out his real name for a long time. For this reason, we had named this tall teacher after his great height: 'Dighol'. Even though we came to know his name later, the tag 'Dighol Sir' stuck.

The topics of our essays changed during his term. The subject of animals was dropped. In its place came tougher topics. I remember that the first essay that Dighol Sir made us write was 'Assam's Natural Beauty.' He let us know, in brief, what the piece should contain, and told us to write those up in our own style. Many could not do so. Instead, they 'repeated' Sir's words. Others copied what the first lot had written. I was very enthusiastic about writing essays, and I would write the substance of what Sir had said in an original way in my own words. Sir never gave us marks. But when he nodded his head and corrected my essay with a tick mark in red ink, I could make out that he quite liked my composition.

More topics followed. Some of them were 'Assam's Natural Resources', 'Floods' and so on. Once, Sir told us to write about 'Our Village'. He told us what the piece should contain. Our house was not exactly in the village, proper. It was a neighbourhood of a few houses clustered around a crossroads with several shops. Because of the marketplace, it had the air of a town, though it was not exactly a town, either. When we were asked to write about our village, I had no way out but to describe the Sunday and Wednesday markets. I was quite nervous when I submitted my copy, afraid that Sir would scold me, saying, 'This is rubbish.' Instead, he looked at me and praised my effort. 'You're beginning to write from your imagination. You should start writing on your own, as well. You'll be able to do it.'

I heard the word 'imagination' for the first time that day.

The topic for the next essay was so difficult that Sir made everybody copy what he himself dictated. The subject was 'Discipline'. We just learnt it off by rote, even though he told us, 'Don't repeat it like parrots. Add a few points of your own.' However, in this essay none of us could add anything to what he said.

One day, Dighol Sir came to the composition class

and said, 'Today I will not give you any subject. Take up any topic, something about what you love. I'll see how proficient you have become in writing. I'll also be able to judge whether you are able to use your imagination. Our school magazine will soon be out. I will put the best essay in the magazine.'

I was filled with enthusiasm on hearing this. But when I returned home, I just could not think of a topic to write about. Every day, my father would sit on the veranda at the back of our house, and read the papers. A particular day's papers would arrive only the next afternoon. After returning from office, Deuta would read the papers from beginning to end before dusk. Deuta would get very annoyed if anybody bothered him during this time. But seeing no way to solve my problem, I approached my father, who was engrossed in reading the papers. On coming to know the reason for this act of mine, my father did not show any anger or annoyance. But he disappointed me by saying, 'Your teacher has asked you to think of a topic and write about it. So if I give you a topic, it won't be yours, will it? Think about something that's close to your heart, something you love, and write about it. If you wish, all right then, I will go over it at night.'

As soon as he said the words 'Something you love,' a subject popped into my mind. Dighol Sir, too, had said that we should write on something that we loved. I thought, why not write on love itself? Perhaps I also wished to startle Sir a bit. The essay that I wrote that day, from my own imagination, was the first original composition of my life, on the topic 'Love'. I am using the word 'original' now, but at that point I had no idea what it was.

I thought that mine was a very good essay. I put in all kinds of things about different kinds of love. I divided love into two categories: superior and inferior. (If Dighol Sir had not been in the habit of using the words 'superior' and 'inferior' quite frequently, they would not have come to my mind at all.) For example, the love of eating, or overeating, could be grouped in the inferior category. Examples of superior love, I wrote, were a mother's love for her children, love of God, and love of one's own country. I placed the love of one's country right at the top, above even the love of God. The reason for this was that Sir had told us the story of Lachit's bravery at the Battle of Saraighat just a few days ago, and I had been totally enthralled by it.

When Sir saw the title of the essay that I submitted to him, he stared at my face for quite a few moments. After reading it, he said, 'You are not yet of the age to know what true love really is. Otherwise, you've written it quite well.'

My essay was not chosen for the magazine. Sir preferred my class friend Nitya's composition to mine. The title of Nitya's essay was 'The Asomiya Language.' I was rather surprised when Nitya's essay was chosen. I was quite certain that all the knowledgeable stuff that he put into his piece was not his own. And indeed, things turned out accordingly. There was a huge fuss as soon as it was published. It was discovered that he had lifted the piece from somewhere else. If it had been me, I would have died of shame. But Nitya was unconcerned. He asked, 'Did you see how I fooled Sir?'

After passing out from school, I entered college. The days of writing essays were past. I was admitted to a college in a large city far away from our place. Nitya studied in a college in a town near our home. I would meet up with him only when I went home during the holidays. I heard that he was a student leader in his college. He learnt how to give speeches relentlessly. It seemed that he was at the forefront of organizing bandhs and dharnas.

On the other hand, I was beginning to write. I had become a target of ridicule for Dighol Sir with my first original essay. But that had not dampened my enthusiasm. My stories and essays appeared in the college magazine. Indeed, a couple of them appeared in the weekly literary supplements of newspapers, as well. I now knew all about love, that topic about which I had been ignorant while at school. But I still thought that Lachit's devotion to his country was a superior love. However, a doubt arose in my mind. I was greatly perturbed by the fact that Lachit Borphukon decapitated his own Mama, his maternal uncle. I thought, could love give rise to so much hate that one could slit one's own uncle's throat? In other words, was there hate on the opposite side of love? This question merely formed itself in my mind. I got no answer to it. Indeed, I can find no answer to it, even now.

Nitya was my friend. When we were in school, I would sometimes go to his home in the village. There was a huge grazing ground that had to be crossed on the way to his village. Once, I had seen a wake of vultures sitting there. It looked as though a group of sweepers was waiting around their red-turbanned leader, getting ready to clear up. Nitya had said, 'They are waiting for a dead cow. Maybe somebody is coming here with one, to dispose of its carcass. Saala,' he swore, 'how do these vultures know about it beforehand?' He had then looked at me and said with a smile, 'Vultures relish dead cattle. Dogs love bones. And what is it that you love, then?' I had realized that he was teasing me about my essay on love. His own plagiarism had not yet been discovered at that time.

It was quite a distance from our neighbourhood to his village. I got thirsty on the way. We entered a migrant cultivator's house and asked for a drink of water. Nitya knew the family. He had said, 'Ilyas is a very good person, you know. He's been living here since my great grandfather's time.' We had rested there on our way back as well.

Nitya was now a student leader in college. We were going our own different ways. Since I was far away from home, I did not get to meet him much. But then the Assam Agitation began, and all studies stopped. There was a battle to be fought to defend the very survival of the people. All selfish aims had to be sacrificed for the sake of this larger goal. The logic of the student leaders was that during the Independence struggle of the country, too, the students had abandoned their studies and jumped into the struggle for Independence.

I returned home. I tried to keep away from the Agitation as much as possible. The student leaders made such fiery speeches that the very air grew heated. Nitya was the leader of our area. His inflammatory speeches aroused blazing passions not just in the students, but also in the minds of older people. Stray incidents of violence began to occur. I stayed at home, away from all of that.

One day, Nitya came over. He asked me, 'You had once written an essay on love, remember?'

'Yes,' I replied.

'You had placed Lachit's love for his motherland right at the top, hadn't you?'

'Indeed, yes,' I said.

'There will be another Saraighat, do you understand? If you love your own people, you must fight this battle.'

I could not deny that I did love the people. I said, 'I support the struggle to protect one's identity. But there's so much conflict…'

He did not allow me to complete my words. 'Keep quiet. If one can go mad for the love of a girl, then one can go wild for the love of one's own people, as well. Those others…those people—you know, those other people—' He did not complete his words. A deep hatred suffused his face, the face of one who loved his own people madly. I could not fail to understand who he meant when he stuttered 'Those people—those other people'.

Looking at me, though, he said, 'It's true that you love your country. But you have no guts. Ok, then stay at home, but if it becomes necessary, you will have to come out and join us. We are all Lachits, we are going out to slash the Mughal soldiers as though they are kosu stems and arum plants. The public is made up of lazy, gutless people like you. At least give us your moral support.'

There were no flames in the air, but it was as hot as a conflagration. Even though I remained at home, Nitya kept telling me every now and again to come out and warm myself at that inferno. On one such day, I accompanied Nitya to his village. This time, I did not see the wake of vultures at the grazing grounds. When I asked Nitya about it, he replied, 'Yes, the vultures have stopped coming here. They bury the cattle that die of foot-and-mouth disease.'

He pointed to a village, which I remembered as Ilyas's. In the past, it had been routine for us to have a drink of water and rest at Ilyas's home. This time, though, Nitya did not go there. I did not go in either. While crossing the grazing field, Nitya gave a significant snigger and said, 'The vultures will return again, understand?'

I was a little surprised. A few days ago, I had read in a magazine that a famous ornithologist had expressed his fear that the number of vultures had declined alarmingly. Like some other kinds of birds, vultures too were probably on the way to extinction. The ornithologist had started specific programmes to revive their numbers, and given advice on ways to preserve the species. Perhaps some programme of this kind had been taken up somewhere around here. Nitya probably knew about it.

Great events sometimes eclipse smaller happenings. Otherwise, why was it that I remained unaware of the incident that should have created a furore in our area? Perhaps that incident had been squashed under the weight of the larger events of the Agitation. An astonishing thing had happened during the period when the Agitation had closed down all academic activity in schools and colleges. Previously, students had obeyed their teachers' instructions. But now the teachers worked according to the dictates of the student leaders, some unwillingly, others quite enthusiastically. Whatever Nitya commanded, came to pass. They would agitate on the orders of the student leaders and join processions. Slogans flashed from the mouths of many of these teachers.

Once, Nitya forced me to join a procession. I noticed that the teachers of our old school followed Nitya's orders implicitly. The veins on their necks swelled up as they joined their voices with great enthusiasm to the slogans that Nitya thundered out in his booming voice. Every now and again, Nitya would bellow out slogans that were communally inflammatory. Our teachers repeated those without any hesitation. I saw only one person who was different. Bapi Sir. I felt that he had come unwillingly. When these slogans were shouted, he kept his mouth shut and looked uncomfortable. I did not see another former teacher of mine. Dighol Sir. I was somewhat surprised. Nitya was the undisputed student leader and it was impossible to disobey him. How could Dighol Sir do so? It was to get to the bottom of this mystery that I turned up that very day at Bapi Sir's place.

It was from him that I learnt about Dighol Sir. I had been unaware that alongside this epic drama of patriotism, the smaller subplot of Dighol Sir's love story was also being played out simultaneously. I had gone away for higher studies to a faraway metro city. It was therefore not at all surprising that I did not get much news of happenings in this remote village. In addition, nobody had the time to discuss the insignificant mudslide created by Dighol Sir, when all around, the Agitation's eye-catchingly novel and original programmes created huge, tumbling erosions every day. This was undoubtedly the reason why nobody from home, not even my father, had thought to give me news of the incident concerning Dighol Sir, caught up as they were in the rush of events. He himself was vociferous in praise of the student leaders, and in learning new lessons on patriotism. He did not deem it necessary to talk about the minor incidents that had taken place in the neighbourhood. Nitya, the student leader, naturally had no time. His fervour of liberating the land had brought a rush of fresh blood to his veins.

I heard Dighol Sir's story from Bapi Sir. I remembered his words when I had submitted my essay on love to him. 'You are not yet of the age to know what true love really is.' Perhaps Sir had left behind, just for me, proof of what true love really was. He had eloped with the daughter of Bhrigu Mahajan, the richest and most economically robust person in our area, and vanished. At that time, Bhrigu Mahajan was not just rich, he was also very powerful, because his son was a magistrate. This son, the magistrate, had already roared that he would see to it that Dighol Sir tasted the meals of a prison. I heard all this from Bapi Sir. His sorrowful eyes were full of sympathy for Dighol Sir.

The atmosphere in our area became even more heated, and I did not have much time to think of Dighol Sir any more. Nitya forced me to join the People's Struggle. Ours was a peaceful agitation. Even so, shops and business establishments were compelled, through force, to remain closed during Bandhs. If somebody did not comply, his shop was shattered by stones that were hurled at it. If long distance trucks came in, unaware of the call for a Bandh, they were set on fire. According to Nitya, we were peaceable. It was the others who were creating the turmoil. Once, Nitya took along a few other boys, and blew up a pipeline that ran through a field. He said, 'Tej Dim, Tel Nidim! We will give up our blood, but not our oil.' But Nitya never had to shed a single drop of blood. Deuta, my father, did not know who blew up the pipeline. Perhaps he had his suspicions. But I saw an expression of pride on Deuta's face at this courageous act.

Once, Nitya appeared at our house at midnight. He seemed very agitated, but there was an expression of satisfaction, too, on his face. He whispered, 'I've finished them all off, you understand? I've burnt them all. The whole village is gone. I chopped up three of them myself.'

My very soul shivered. I asked, 'You've killed people, humans?'

He replied, 'I haven't killed any humans. I have destroyed the enemy. This is a second Saraighat. It's Do or Die.'

I asked, 'Which village?'

He replied, 'That one,' and pointed towards the direction in which lay Ilyas's village, the same village where Nitya would rest, and have a drink of water, while coming and going. Out of love for his country, Lachit had executed his uncle in that first Battle of Saraighat. It was the enemy, merely, who had been hacked to pieces during this Second Sariaghat. There was so much hatred mingled with Nitya's love for his motherland that his conscience did not protest when he attacked the village with whose people he had lived in brotherly amity for such a long time. He slept at our house quite without a care, as though he was a famished demon who had just assuaged his hunger. Next day, I got to know that Ilyas's entire family had been wiped out by Nitya's patriotic fervour.

I understood, now, the significance of what Nitya had said when we had gone that last time to his village. When I had commented on the fact that there were no vultures to be seen, he had replied, 'The vultures will return.'

I was burnt by flames of remorse. There was so much blood flowing from the word 'Love' that I was afraid I would drown and be suffocated by it. I left my home. Before that, I had learned from Bapi Sir that Bhrigu Maharaj's magistrate son had got Dighol Sir arrested. When I left my village, Dighol Sir was in jail. Bhrigu Mahajan married off his daughter to some other bridegroom, along with a fat dowry of much money, property and land, and thus freed her from the stigma of her kidnapping. The girl, I heard, came forward for the wedding without protest of any kind.

The news of the Second Battle of Saraighat waged against the enemy soldiers, that is, against Ilyas and his villagers, did not manage to grab newspaper headlines. For even more major battles were taking place at the same time: in Nellie, Saulkhowa, Mukalmuwa, Gohpur. Some enthusiastic journalist got a whiff of Hitler's 'Final Solution' in these incidents.

However, Nitya himself could not develop into a petty Hitler, for there were other valiant heroes who were able to organize incidents that were much bigger. Actually, the journalist had interpreted events wrongly. Hitler had preached the concept of the Final Solution through the use of government machinery, and the intellectuals of the time, puffed up with national pride, had supported him silently. Nitya and his companions did not control government machinery. But like Hitler, through their oratory, they had forged a potent weapon using the people themselves.

I kept thinking of all this. There was no way I could articulate my thoughts out loud. For I had heard that those 'anti-Assamese' people who had spoken out had had their faces smashed, their homes ransacked. They had been publicly humiliated by being forced to clutch their ears and kneel on the ground, as though they were small children being punished.

The newspapers were on fire. Blazing words became inextricably mingled with thick clots of blood. A new genre of journalism was born. At that very time, I don't really know how, a small news item appeared as a boxed item on the front page. Perhaps the news editor of the paper had felt the need for a different type of horror story in order to break the monotony of the news that was appearing all the time. I was astounded by the headline. 'Uproar on Chandmari footpath: frenzied man kills former girlfriend.' Dighol Sir's name was mentioned. Dighol Sir had fallen into a frenzy on seeing his former lover walking with her husband, and knifed her.

That day, I remembered once more, my essay on 'Love.' I had known nothing about love at that time. How could I have known, at that age, about the huge measure of hate that was heaped on love? I remembered, too, Nitya's face, wild with love for his motherland. Hate and satisfaction had mingled in that face after he had returned from killing those people. Nitya's acts frightened me. I was saddened by Dighol Sir's changed condition. Later, I learnt from Bapi Sir, that Dighol Sir had become insane. He was an inmate of the lunatic asylum. Otherwise, he would surely have been hanged.

I should have been surprised when Nitya became the Deputy Superintendent of Police, but wasn't. The political landscape had changed very fast. The leaders of the Agitation now controlled the fate of the state and its people. Nitya had only been a petty student leader in a regional organization. The fruits of his sacrifice were therefore somewhat diminutive. I heard that he had become a proficient officer. His ability to keep the law and order situation under control had earned him the charge of important cities. He was successful in showing his skill in ramming apart agitators and protesting crowds by using road rollers. Like the fellow students of the past, now the ministers of the day reposed trust in him and his beautiful, two-storied mansion rose swiftly in an exclusive area of the city.

I had quietly started my teaching career by then. He had not, however, forgotten me. He would welcome me as a friend. Of course, there was no opportunity for meeting up every day. He was a busy officer at the Sub-Divisional Headquarters. I was a teacher in a venture college located in the backwaters of a nearby town.

Bit by bit, though, the euphoria of my one-time co-student, once a student leader, enthroned now in a position of power, began to be punctured. Like small doses of medicine, some bombs began to explode here and there. This was another reason for Nitya's hectic schedule. He was also responsible for searching out those traitors and putting a stop to their deeds. It appeared that he set about this task with a great deal of enthusiasm. Before his expertise, no strapping youth who was suspected to be involved in terrorism could remain unharmed. He stamped his mark on them as though they were animals being branded, and inflicted permanent imprints on their bodies. It is not known whether the real terrorists were terrorized by this anti-terror tactic. But these branded youths began to flee their hearths and homes.

It was during that time that a middle-aged woman came to me. It appeared that she had heard that Nitya was my friend. I was in a dilemma. She had come to request me to use my influence to get Nitya to release her young son, whom he had taken into custody from his house the previous evening. She had heard that a couple of boys, whom Nitya had detained by night in a similar manner, had never returned home at all.

The woman's importunate pleas forced me to approach Nitya. He received me very warmly and with courtesy. I broached the subject. The same Nitya who had sacrificed himself for patriotism now growled, 'Ok, it's those people. Saala, they pose as patriots! I'll make them puke out their patriotism...'

I told him, 'He's innocent.'

'Innocent?' he asked. 'How can you know that? Have you seen him, saala, he looks like a bull.'

I was at a loss to understand the link between terror and a physique like a bull's. I tried to make him believe in the boy's innocence. In the end, 'for the sake of our friendship,' he agreed. He told me to send the mother to him.

A few days later, the mother came to me again, to express her gratitude. With a wan smile, she informed me that her son had been set free. 'Bopai, the whole affair was done without much difficulty only because you intervened. It didn't cost us as much as it would have otherwise. We gave him the ten thousand rupees from my husband's pension.' I could quite understand which way the needle of Nitya 'carrying out his responsibilities' now pointed.

Now why am I thinking of writing another essay on love? As a child, I had wanted to write on love to startle Dighol Sir. At that time, I had not yet understood the meaning of love. I understand it now. There is a recipient of my love now. But I have not yet been able to tell her clearly my feelings for her. She is becoming doubtful about my love. I am becoming doubtful about the word 'love' itself. I have seen Nitya's love for his people in the past, mixed with hatred. And now, I have seen his love for his responsibilities, mingled with arrogance. I have heard about Dighol Sir's maniacal love, mixed with hate. Nitya's love had shown me the Veer Rasa, a heroic emotion, mixed with a kind of absurdity. Dighol Sir's love had shown me Karuna Rasa, an emotion of pity and sadness. I cannot utter this word that denotes love mixed with hate to the object of my love. This is why, by writing this, I am trying to expel the blood of hatred that is mingled with the word Love for me. I am trying to purify the word 'love' itself. Let the object of my love understand my feelings on reading this essay. Let her understand, also, why I do not consider the word 'love' to be a suitable vehicle to convey my feelings to her.

But what is this? Where is the serial plot? Have I morphed into a Disappointed Lover? No, I have not become rapt only in contemplation of the object of my love. I have also become socially aware. I am environmentally conscious. I have already written about an ornithologist expressing his fear that the entire vulture species was on the verge of extinction. The other day, I came upon yet another detailed article that he had written.

Marshalling statistics and data, he was able to prove that two kinds of vultures have already become extinct by now. He gave photographs as well. Because my environmental awareness had improved, I was disturbed when I read this. The avian expert did not pinpoint the reasons for these two varieties of vultures becoming extinct. But I feel that they are not getting enough food. They like feeding on dead animals, and also on human corpses. Recently, the government published statistics showing that during their tenure, both animals and humans have become healthier. The death rate has decreased. Man and beast are both living longer. Where then can vultures get their food from?

It was because I had been thinking along these lines that one day, when I saw a rare vulture that the ornithologist had declared extinct, sitting on the leafless branch of a very tall silk cotton tree, I stood still and gazed happily at the bird. I regretted that I did not have a camera handy with which to take a picture and send to the avian expert. Previously, I had thought the vulture to be an ugly bird. But that day, I felt some kind of affection for the bird, and I thought she was beautiful.

A person who had become an acquaintance during my regular morning walks saw me looking raptly at the branch of the tree. He asked, 'What are you looking at?' He could not understand that there could be something worth seeing on that huge, bare tree. I pointed out the vulture to him. Perhaps he was surprised at my fascination, for he said, 'Maybe somebody has tossed a dead cow or something nearby. If that's the case, a few more of them will appear. But the way you have been staring at it so intently, I thought you'd seen something very valuable.'

On hearing his opinion, I said, 'Research has shown that this beautiful bird, so useful for humans, is now extinct. This sight is therefore quite rare. Isn't it beautiful?'

He grew suspicious on hearing me use the word 'beautiful', and continued on his way.

The object of my love is beautiful. I had said that the vulture was beautiful. I had got that feeling as soon as I had spotted that rare bird. Had I then diminished my lover's beauty? Or perhaps the word 'beauty' itself had acquired another meaning, another dimension, as a marker of the attribute?

But I did not have time to ponder on all this. For when I returned home, I heard that dangerous enemies had flung a grenade at the 'invincible officer', my friend Nitya, wounding him. Though not in any imminent danger of departing from this life, he was badly injured on his calves, hands and back. I rushed out to see him at the Sub-Divisional Headquarters. If I went to the station immediately, I would be able to catch a train for his place. I hurriedly caught an auto and alighted outside the station. There I saw an unshaven, unkempt man with long, rough hair, wandering around aimlessly. Suddenly, the man looked at me. I seemed to recognize the man's eyes even through his dishevelled looks. Dighol Sir! He too seemed to recognize me. He promptly turned his face away and began to forage in the only dustbin outside the station.

I remember clearly that it was at that very moment that there was a terrible blast. And in the explosion, the shattered body of the person whom I had taken to be Dighol Sir was flung in many pieces. The explosion was so powerful that one of the man's severed hands was hurled against the station clock with such force that it buckled and bent. Even if I joined all those pieces of flesh together, I would not be able to determine whether this really had been Dighol Sir or not. But the thought occurred to me that this person, who had been maddened with love, and the bomb which had reduced his body to smithereens, had together sent out a double message: the message of patriotism and hatred for mankind, mingled together. That message knocked at the trembling in my heart, making it beat loud and fast.

At that moment, I saw in my mind that same vulture which I had earlier spotted on the bare branch of the huge silk cotton tree. After getting a whiff of the food it loved, it was now circling the sky above me with an ugly enthusiasm. It was no longer alone. Several other vultures had joined it. But was there any food available for them in these scattered pieces of flesh?

What kind of an essay on love is this? Aren't the markers of love themselves repeatedly prodding and stabbing me? Also, by coincidence, Dighol Sir's wild love has been bonded with the frenzied patriotism of that unknown youth who had placed that bomb in the dustbin. But is it coincidence, or dissonance? Synchronous or discordant? Has this composite raaga degenerated into a jarring strain because of this fractured rhythm?

This essay on love is without meaning or significance. I shall not be able to offer this essay to the object of my love as a sign of my affections. I am therefore presenting this to you as pieces of a tale from a generic narrative. By listening to the mixed melodies of the frenzy of love, the madness of hate, and the lunacy of violence, you can decide whether or not the word 'love' has been shattered in the storm of the several components that make up the word itself.

Acknowledgements

To the author himself, Harekrishna Deka, for entrusting me with these stories to translate, and not interfering at all with the process, and having faith in me through all these years!

To Speaking Tiger Books, and Ravi Singh, for giving translations from Indian languages to English this space, for making available some of the best works in these languages to the English language reader through translations.

To my editor, Sudeshna Shome Ghosh, for the meticulous reading of the text, and for her invaluable suggestions.

To my late parents, Pramod and Geeta Goswami, who were my go-to consultants regarding the Assamese language while they were alive. Their readily rendered help made the work much easier for me to complete, in the earlier years.